THE MAN WHO SHOT LIBERTY VALANCE

Center Point
Large Print

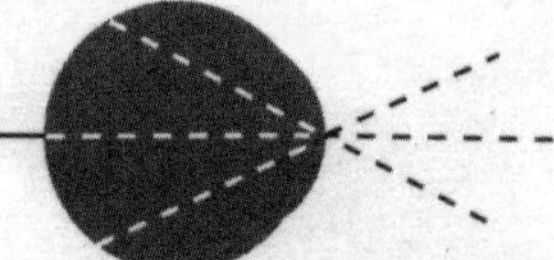

This Large Print Book carries the Seal of Approval of N.A.V.H.

The Man Who Shot Liberty Valance

and

A Man Called Horse
Lost Sister
The Hanging Tree

Dorothy M. Johnson

Center Point Publishing
Thorndike, Maine

This Center Point Large Print edition
is published in the year 2006 by arrangement with
McIntosh and Otis, Inc.

The text of this Large Print edition is unabridged. In other aspects, this book may vary from the original edition. Printed in Thailand. Set in 16-point Times New Roman type.

ISBN 1-58547-709-5

Library of Congress Cataloging-in-Publication Data

Johnson, Dorothy M.
The man who shot Liberty Valance / Dorothy M. Johnson.--Center Point large print ed.
p. cm.
ISBN 1-58547-709-5 (lib. bdg. : alk. paper)
1. Large type books. I. Title.

PS3519.O233M36 2006
813'.54--dc22

2005021624

Contents

A Man Called Horse

He was a young man of good family, as the phrase went in the New England of a hundred-odd years ago, and the reasons for his bitter discontent were unclear, even to himself. He grew up in the gracious old Boston home under his grandmother's care, for his mother had died in giving him birth; and all his life he had known every comfort and privilege his father's wealth could provide.

But still there was the discontent, which puzzled him because he could not even define it. He wanted to live among his equals—people who were no better than he and no worse either. That was as close as he could come to describing the source of his unhappiness in Boston and his restless desire to go somewhere else.

In the year 1845, he left home and went out West, far beyond the country's creeping frontier, where he hoped to find his equals. He had the idea that in Indian country, where there was danger, all white men were kings, and he wanted to be one of them. But he found, in the West as in Boston, that the men he respected were still his superiors, even if they could not read, and those he did not respect weren't worth talking to.

He did have money, however, and he could hire the men he respected. He hired four of them, to cook and hunt and guide and be his companions, but he found them not friendly.

They were apart from him and he was still alone. He still brooded about his status in the world, longing for his equals.

On a day in June, he learned what it was to have no status at all. He became a captive of a small raiding party of Crow Indians.

He heard gunfire and the brief shouts of his companions around the bend of the creek just before they died, but he never saw their bodies. He had no chance to fight, because he was naked and unarmed, bathing in the creek, when a Crow warrior seized and held him.

His captor let him go at last, let him run. Then the lot of them rode him down for sport, striking him with their coup sticks. They carried the dripping scalps of his companions, and one had skinned off Baptiste's black beard as well, for a trophy.

They took him along in a matter-of-fact way, as they took the captured horses. He was unshod and naked as the horses were, and like them he had a rawhide thong around his neck. So long as he didn't fall down, the Crows ignored him.

On the second day they gave him his breeches. His feet were too swollen for his boots, but one of the Indians threw him a pair of moccasins that had belonged to the halfbreed, Henri, who was dead back at the creek. The captive wore the moccasins gratefully. The third day they let him ride one of the spare horses so the party could move faster, and on that day they came in sight of their camp.

He thought of trying to escape, hoping he might be killed in flight rather than by slow torture in the camp, but he never had a chance to try. They were more familiar with escape than he was and, knowing what to expect, they forestalled it. The only other time he had tried to escape from anyone, he had succeeded. When he had left his home in Boston, his father had raged and his grandmother had cried, but they could not talk him out of his intention.

The men of the Crow raiding party didn't bother with talk.

Before riding into camp they stopped and dressed in their regalia, and in parts of their victims' clothing; they painted their faces black. Then, leading the white man by the rawhide around his neck as though he were a horse, they rode down toward the tepee circle, shouting and singing, brandishing their weapons. He was unconscious when they got there; he fell and was dragged.

He lay dazed and battered near a tepee while the noisy, busy life of the camp swarmed around him and Indians came to stare. Thirst consumed him, and when it rained he lapped rain water from the ground like a dog. A scrawny, shrieking, eternally busy old woman with ragged graying hair threw a chunk of meat on the grass, and he fought the dogs for it.

When his head cleared, he was angry, although anger was an emotion he knew he could not afford.

It was better when I was a horse, he thought—when they led me by the rawhide around my neck. I won't be a dog, no matter what!

The hag gave him stinking, rancid grease and let him figure out what it was for. He applied it gingerly to his bruised and sun-seared body.

Now, he thought, I smell like the rest of them.

While he was healing, he considered coldly the advantages of being a horse. A man would be humiliated, and sooner or later he would strike back and that would be the end of him. But a horse had only to be docile. Very well, he would learn to do without pride.

He understood that he was the property of the screaming old woman, a fine gift from her son, one that she liked to show off. She did more yelling at him than at anyone else, probably to impress the neighbors so they would not forget what a great and generous man her son was. She was bossy and proud, a dreadful sag of skin and bones, and she was a devilish hard worker.

The white man, who now thought of himself as a horse, forgot sometimes to worry about his danger. He kept making mental notes of things to tell his own people in Boston about this hideous adventure. He would go back a hero, and he would say, "Grandmother, let me fetch your shawl. I've been accustomed to doing little errands for another lady about your age."

Two girls lived in the tepee with the old hag and her warrior son. One of them, the white man concluded, was his captor's wife and the other was his little sister. The daughter-in-law was smug and spoiled. Being beloved, she did not have to be useful. The younger girl had bright, wandering eyes. Often enough they wandered to the white man who was pretending to be a horse.

The two girls worked when the old woman put them at it, but they were always running off to do something they enjoyed more. There were games and noisy contests, and there was much laughter. But not for the white man. He was finding out what loneliness could be.

That was a rich summer on the plains, with plenty of buffalo for meat and clothing and the making of tepees. The Crows were wealthy in horses, prosperous and contented. If their men had not been so avid for glory, the white man thought, there would have been a lot more of them. But they went out of their way to court death, and when one of them met it, the whole camp mourned extravagantly and cried to their God for vengeance.

The captive was a horse all summer, a docile bearer of burdens, careful and patient. He kept reminding himself that he had to be better-natured than other horses, because he could not lash out with hoofs or teeth. Helping the old woman load up the horses for travel, he yanked at a pack and said, "Whoa, brother. It goes easier when you don't fight."

The horse gave him a big-eyed stare as if it understood his language—a comforting thought, because nobody else did. But even among the horses he felt unequal. They were able to look out for themselves if they escaped. He would simply starve. He was envious still, even among the horses.

Humbly he fetched and carried. Sometimes he even offered to help, but he had not the skill for the endless work of the women, and he was not trusted to hunt with the men, the providers.

When the camp moved, he carried a pack trudging with the women. Even the dogs worked then, pulling small burdens on travois of sticks.

The Indian who had captured him lived like a lord, as he had a right to do. He hunted with his peers, attended long ceremonial meetings with much chanting and dancing, and lounged in the shade with his smug bride. He had only two responsibilities: to kill buffalo and to gain glory. The white man was so far beneath him in status that the Indian did not even think of envy.

One day several things happened that made the captive think he might sometime become a man again. That was the day when he began to understand their language. For four months he had heard it, day and night, the joy and the mourning, the ritual chanting and sung prayers, the squabbles and the deliberations. None of it meant anything to him at all.

But on that important day in early fall the two young women set out for the river, and one of them called over her shoulder to the old woman. The white man was startled. She had said she was going to bathe. His understanding was so sudden that he felt as if his ears had come unstopped. Listening to the racket of the camp, he heard fragments of meaning instead of gabble.

On that same important day the old woman brought a pair of new moccasins out of the tepee and tossed them on the ground before him. He could not believe she would do anything for him because of kindness, but giving him moccasins was one way of looking after her property.

In thanking her, he dared greatly. He picked a little handful of fading fall flowers and took them to her as she squatted in front of her tepee, scraping a buffalo hide with a tool made from a piece of iron tied to a bone. Her hands were hideous—most of the fingers had the first joint missing. He bowed solemnly and offered the flowers.

She glared at him from beneath the short, ragged tangle of her hair. She stared at the flowers, knocked them out of his hand and went running to the next tepee, squalling the story. He heard her and the other women screaming with laughter.

The white man squared his shoulders and walked boldly over to watch three small boys shooting arrows at a target. He said in English, "Show me how to do that, will you?"

They frowned, but he held out his hand as if there could be no doubt. One of them gave him a bow and one arrow, and they snickered when he missed.

The people were easily amused, except when they were angry. They were amused, at him, playing with the little boys. A few days later he asked the hag, with gestures, for a bow that her son had just discarded, a man-size bow of horn. He scavenged for old arrows. The old woman cackled at his marksmanship and called her neighbors to enjoy the fun.

When he could understand words, he could identify his people by their names. The old woman was Greasy Hand, and her daughter was Pretty Calf. The other young woman's name was not clear to him, for the words were not in his vocabulary. The man who had captured him was Yellow Robe.

Once he could understand, he could begin to talk a little, and then he was less lonely. Nobody had been able to see any reason for talking to him, since he would not understand anyway. He asked the old woman, "What is my name?" Until he knew it, he was incomplete. She shrugged to let him know he had none.

He told her in the Crow language, "My name is Horse." He repeated it, and she nodded. After that they called him Horse when they called him anything. Nobody cared except the white man himself.

They trusted him enough to let him stray out of camp, so that he might have got away and, by unimaginable good luck, might have reached a trading post or a fort, but winter was too close. He did not dare leave without a horse; he needed clothing and a better hunting weapon than he had, and more certain skill in using it. He did not dare steal, for then they would surely have pursued him, and just as certainly they would have caught him. Remembering the warmth of the home that was waiting in Boston, he settled down for the winter.

On a cold night he crept into the tepee after the others had gone to bed. Even a horse might try to find shelter from the wind. The old woman grumbled, but without conviction. She did not put him out.

They tolerated him, back in the shadows, so long as he did not get in the way.

He began to understand how the family that owned him differed from the others. Fate had been cruel to them. In a short, sharp argument among the old women, one of them derided Greasy Hand by sneering, "You have no relatives!" and Greasy Hand raved for minutes of the deeds of her father and uncles and brothers. And she had had four sons, she reminded her detractor—who answered with scorn, "Where are they?"

Later the white man found her moaning and whimpering to herself, rocking back and forth on her haunches, staring at her mutilated hands. By that time he understood. A mourner often chopped off a finger joint. Old Greasy Hand had mourned often. For the first time he felt a twinge of pity, but he put it aside as another emotion, like anger, that he could not afford. He thought: What tales I will tell when I get home!

He wrinkled his nose in disdain. The camp stank of animals and meat and rancid grease. He looked down at his naked, shivering legs and was startled, remembering that he was still only a horse.

He could not trust the old woman. She fed him only because a starved slave would die and not be worth boasting about. Just how fitful her temper was he saw on the day when she got tired of stumbling over one of the hundred dogs that infested the camp. This was one of her own dogs, a large, strong one that pulled a baggage travois when the tribe moved camp.

Countless times he had seen her kick at the beast as it lay sleeping in front of the tepee, in her way. The dog always moved, with a yelp, but it always got in the way again. One day she gave the dog its usual kick and then stood scolding at it while the animal rolled its eyes sleepily. The old woman suddenly picked up her axe and cut the dog's head off with one blow. Looking well satisfied with herself, she beckoned her slave to remove the body.

It could have been me, he thought, if I were a dog. But I'm a horse.

His hope of life lay with the girl, Pretty Calf. He set about courting her, realizing how desperately poor he was both in property and honor. He owned no horse, no weapon but the old bow and the battered arrows. He had nothing to give away, and he needed gifts, because he did not dare seduce the girl.

One of the customs of courtship involved sending a gift of horses to a girl's older brother and bestowing much buffalo meat upon her mother. The white man could not wait for some far-off time when he might have either horses or meat to give away. And his courtship had to be secret. It was not for him to stroll past the groups of watchful girls, blowing a flute made of an eagle's wing bone, as the flirtatious young bucks did.

He could not ride past Pretty Calf's tepee, painted and bedizened; he had no horse, no finery.

Back home, he remembered, I could marry just about any girl I'd want to. But he wasted little time thinking about that. A future was something to be earned.

The most he dared do was wink at Pretty Calf now and then, or state his admiration while she giggled and hid her face. The least he dared do to win his bride was to elope with her, but he had to give her a horse to put the seal of tribal approval on that. And he had no horse until he killed a man to get one. . . .

His opportunity came in early spring. He was casually accepted by that time. He did not belong, but he was amusing to the Crows, like a strange pet, or they would not have fed him through the winter.

His chance came when he was hunting small game with three young boys who were his guards as well as his scornful companions. Rabbits and birds were of no account in a camp well fed on buffalo meat, but they made good targets.

His party walked far that day. All of them at once saw the two horses in a sheltered coulee. The boys and the man crawled forward on their bellies, and then they saw an Indian who lay on the ground, moaning, a lone traveler. From the way the boys inched eagerly forward, Horse knew the man was fair prey—a member of some enemy tribe.

This is the way the captive white man acquired wealth and honor to win a bride and save his life: He shot an arrow into the sick man, a split second ahead of one of his small companions, and dashed forward to strike the still-groaning man with his bow, to count first coup. Then he seized the hobbled horses.

By the time he had the horses secure, and with them his hope for freedom, the boys had followed, counting coup with gestures and shrieks they had practiced since boyhood, and one of them had the scalp. The white man was grimly amused to see the boy double up with sudden nausea when he had the thing in his hand. . . .

There was a hubbub in the camp when they rode in that evening, two of them on each horse. The captive was noticed. Indians who had ignored him as a slave stared at the brave man who had struck first coup and had stolen horses.

The hubbub lasted all night, as fathers boasted loudly of their young sons' exploits. The white man was called upon to settle an argument between two fierce boys as to which of them had struck second coup and which must be satisfied with third. After much talk that went over his head, he solemnly pointed at the nearest boy. He didn't know which boy it was and didn't care, but the boy did.

The white man had watched warriors in their triumph. He knew what to do. Modesty about achievements had no place among the Crow people. When a man did something big, he told about it.

The white man smeared his face with grease and charcoal. He walked inside the tepee circle, chanting and singing. He used his own language.

"You heathens, you savages," he shouted. "I'm going to get out of here someday! I am going to get away!" The Crow people listened respectfully. In the Crow tongue he shouted, "Horse! I am Horse!" and they nodded.

He had a right to boast, and he had two horses. Before dawn, the white man and his bride were sheltered beyond a far hill, and he was telling her, "I love you, little lady. I love you."

She looked at him with her great dark eyes, and he thought she understood his English words—or as much as she needed to understand.

"You are my treasure," he said, "more precious than jewels, better than fine gold. I am going to call you Freedom."

When they returned to camp two days later, he was bold but worried. His ace, he suspected, might not be high enough in the game he was playing without being sure of the rifles. But it served.

Old Greasy Hand raged—but not at him. She complained loudly that her daughter had let herself go too cheap. But the marriage was as good as any Crow marriage. He had paid a horse.

He learned the language faster after that, from Pretty Calf, whom he sometimes called Freedom. He learned that his attentive, adoring bride was fourteen years old.

One thing he had not guessed was the difference that being Pretty Calf's husband would make in his relationship to her mother and brother. He had hoped only to make his position a little safer, but he had not expected to be treated with dignity. Greasy Hand no longer spoke to him at all. When the white man spoke to her, his bride murmured in dismay, explaining at great length that he must never do that. There could be no conversation between a man and his mother-in-law. He could not even mention a word that was part of her name.

Having improved his status so magnificently, he felt no need for hurry in getting away. Now that he had a woman, he had as good a chance to be rich as any man. Pretty Calf waited on him; she seldom ran off to play games with other young girls, but took pride in learning from her mother the many women's skills of tanning hides and making clothing and preparing food.

He was no more a horse but a kind of man, a half-Indian, still poor and unskilled but laden with honors, clinging to the buckskin fringes of Crow society.

Escape could wait until he could manage it in comfort, with fit clothing and a good horse, with hunting weapons. Escape could wait until the camp moved near some trading post. He did not plan how he would get home. He dreamed of being there all at once, and of telling stories nobody would believe. There was no hurry.

Pretty Calf delighted in educating him. He began to understand tribal arrangements, customs and why things were as they were. They were that way because they had always been so. His young wife giggled when she told him, in his ignorance, things she had always known. But she did not laugh when her brother's wife was taken by another warrior. She explained that solemnly with words and signs.

Yellow Robe belonged to a society called the Big Dogs. The wife stealer, Cut Neck, belonged to the Foxes. They were fellow tribesmen; they hunted together and fought side by side, but men of one society could take away wives from the other society if they wished, subject to certain limitations.

When Cut Neck rode up to the tepee, laughing and singing, and called to Yellow Robe's wife, "Come out! Come out!" she did as ordered, looking smug as usual, meek and entirely willing. Thereafter she rode beside him in ceremonial processions and carried his coup stick, while his other wife pretended not to care.

"But why?" the white man demanded of his wife, his Freedom. "Why did our brother let his woman go? He sits and smokes and does not speak."

Pretty Calf was shocked at the suggestion. Her brother could not possibly reclaim his woman, she explained. He could not even let her come back if she wanted to—and she probably would want to when Cut

Neck tired of her. Yellow Robe could not even admit that his heart was sick. That was the way things were. Deviation meant dishonor.

The woman could have hidden from Cut Neck, she said. She could even have refused to go with him if she had been *ba-wurokee*—a really virtuous woman. But she had been his woman before, for a little while on a berrying expedition, and he had a right to claim her.

There was no sense in it, the white man insisted. He glared at his young wife. "If you go, I will bring you back!" he promised.

She laughed and buried her head against his shoulder. "I will not have to go," she said. "Horse is my first man. There is no hole in my moccasin."

He stroked her hair and said, *"Ba-wurokee."*

With great daring, she murmured, *"Hayha,"* and when he did not answer, because he did not know what she meant, she drew away, hurt.

"A woman calls her man that if she thinks he will not leave her. Am I wrong?"

The white man held her closer and lied. "Pretty Calf is not wrong. Horse will not leave her. Horse will not take another woman, either." No, he certainly would not. Parting from this one was going to be harder than getting her had been. *"Hayha,"* he murmured. "Freedom."

His conscience irked him, but not very much. Pretty Calf could get another man easily enough when he was gone, and a better provider. His hunting skill was improving, but he was still awkward.

There was no hurry about leaving. He was used to most of the Crow ways and could stand the rest. He was becoming prosperous. He owned five horses. His place in the life of the tribe was secure, such as it was. Three or four young women, including the one who had belonged to Yellow Robe, made advances to him. Pretty Calf took pride in the fact that her man was so attractive.

By the time he had what he needed for a secret journey, the grass grew yellow on the plains and the long cold was close. He was enslaved by the girl he called Freedom and, before the winter ended, by the knowledge that she was carrying his child. . . .

The Big Dog society held a long ceremony in the spring. The white man strolled with his woman along the creek bank, thinking: When I get home I will tell them about the chants and the drumming. Sometime. Sometime.

Pretty Calf would not go to bed when they went back to the tepee.

"Wait and find out about my brother," she urged. "Something may happen."

So far as Horse could figure out, the Big Dogs were having some kind of election. He pampered his wife by staying up with her by the fire. Even the old woman, who was a great one for getting sleep when she was not working, prowled around restlessly.

The white man was yawning by the time the noise of the ceremony died down. When Yellow Robe strode in, garish and heathen in his paint and feathers and furs, the women cried out. There was conversation, too fast for Horse to follow, and the old woman wailed once, but her son silenced her with a gruff command.

When the white man went to sleep, he thought his wife was weeping beside him.

The next morning she explained.

"He wears the bearskin belt. Now he can never retreat in battle. He will always be in danger. He will die."

Maybe he wouldn't, the white man tried to convince her. Pretty Calf recalled that some few men had been honored by the bearskin belt, vowed to the highest daring, and had not died. If they lived through the summer, then they were free of it.

"My brother wants to die," she mourned. "His heart is bitter."

Yellow Robe lived through half a dozen clashes with small parties of raiders from hostile tribes. His honors were many. He captured horses in an enemy camp, led two successful raids, counted first coup and snatched a gun from the hand of an enemy tribesman. He wore wolf tails on his moccasins and ermine skins on his shirt, and he fringed his leggings with scalps in token of his glory.

When his mother ventured to suggest, as she did many times, "My son should take a new wife, I need another woman to help me," he ignored her. He spent much time in prayer, alone in the hills or in conference with a medicine man. He fasted and made vows and kept them. And before he could be free of the heavy honor of the bearskin belt, he went on his last raid.

The warriors were returning from the north just as the white man and two other hunters approached from the south, with buffalo and elk meat dripping from the bloody hides tied on their restive ponies. One of the hunters grunted, and they stopped to watch a rider on the hill north of the tepee circle.

The rider dismounted, held up a blanket and dropped it. He repeated the gesture.

The hunters murmured dismay. "Two! Two men dead!" They rode fast into the camp, where there was already wailing.

A messenger came down from the war party on the hill. The rest of the party delayed to paint their faces for mourning and for victory. One of the two dead men was Yellow Robe. They had put his body in a cave and walled it in with rocks. The other man died later, and his body was in a tree.

There was blood on the ground before the tepee to which Yellow Robe would return no more. His mother, with her hair chopped short, sat in the doorway, rocking back and forth on her haunches, wailing her heartbreak. She cradled one mutilated hand in the other. She had cut off another finger joint.

Pretty Calf had cut off chunks of her long hair and was crying as she gashed her arms with a knife. The white man tried to take the knife away, but she protested so piteously that he let her do as she wished. He was sickened with the lot of them.

Savages! he thought. Now I will go back! I'll go hunting alone, and I'll keep on going.

But he did not go just yet, because he was the only hunter in the lodge of the two grieving women, one of them old and the other pregnant with his child.

In their mourning, they made him a pauper again. Everything that meant comfort, wealth and safety they sacrificed to the spirits because of the death of Yellow Robe. The tepee, made of seventeen fine buffalo hides, the furs that should have kept them warm, the white deerskin dress, trimmed with elk teeth, that Pretty Calf loved so well, even their tools and Yellow Robe's weapons—everything but his sacred medicine objects—they left there on the prairie, and the whole camp moved away. Two of his best horses were killed as a sacrifice, and the women gave away the rest.

They had no shelter. They would have no tepee of their own for two months at least of mourning, and then the women would have to tan hides to make it. Meanwhile they could live in temporary huts made of willows, covered with skins given them in pity by their friends. They could have lived with relatives, but Yellow Robe's women had no relatives.

The white man had not realized until then how terrible a thing it was for a Crow to have no kinfolk. No wonder old Greasy Hand had only stumps for fingers. She had mourned, from one year to the next, for everyone she had ever loved. She had no one left but her daughter, Pretty Calf.

Horse was furious at their foolishness. It had been

bad enough for him, a captive, to be naked as a horse and poor as a slave, but that was because his captors had stripped him. These women had voluntarily given up everything they needed.

He was too angry at them to sleep in the willow hut. He lay under a sheltering tree. And on the third night of the mourning he made his plans. He had a knife and a bow. He would go after meat, taking two horses. And he would not come back. There were, he realized, many things he was not going to tell when he got back home.

In the willow hut, Pretty Calf cried out. He heard rustling there, and the old woman's querulous voice.

Some twenty hours later his son was born, two months early, in the tepee of a skilled medicine woman. The child was born without breath, and the mother died before the sun went down.

The white man was too shocked to think whether he should mourn, or how he should mourn. The old woman screamed until she was voiceless. Piteously she approached him, bent and trembling, blind with grief. She held out her knife and he took it.

She spread out her hands and shook her head. If she cut off any more finger joints, she could do no more work. She could not afford any more lasting signs of grief.

The white man said, "All right! All right!" between his teeth. He hacked his arms with the knife and stood watching the blood run down. It was little enough to do for Pretty Calf, for little Freedom.

Now there is nothing to keep me, he realized. When I get home, I must not let them see the scars.

He looked at Greasy Hand, hideous in her grief-burdened age, and thought: I really am free now! When a wife dies, her husband has no more duty toward her family. Pretty Calf had told him so, long ago, when he wondered why a certain man moved out of one tepee and into another.

The old woman, of course, would be a scavenger. There was one other with the tribe, an ancient crone who had no relatives, toward whom no one felt any responsibility. She lived on food thrown away by the more fortunate. She slept in shelters that she built with her own knotted hands. She plodded wearily at the end of the procession when the camp moved. When she stumbled, nobody cared. When she died, nobody would miss her.

Tomorrow morning, the white man decided, I will go.

His mother-in-law's sunken mouth quivered. She said one word, questioningly. She said, *"Eero-oshay?"* She said, "Son?"

Blinking, he remembered. When a wife died, her husband was free. But her mother, who had ignored him with dignity, might if she wished ask him to stay. She invited him by calling him Son, and he accepted by answering Mother.

Greasy Hand stood before him, bowed with years, withered with unceasing labor, loveless and childless, scarred with grief. But with all her burdens, she still loved life enough to beg it from him, the only person she had any right to ask. She was stripping herself of all she had left, her pride.

He looked eastward across the prairie. Two thousand miles away was home. The old woman would not live forever. He could afford to wait, for he was young. He could afford to be magnanimous, for he knew he was a man. He gave her the answer. *"Eegya,"* he said. "Mother."

He went home three years later. He explained no more than to say, "I lived with Crows for a while. It was some time before I could leave. They called me Horse."

He did not find it necessary either to apologize or to boast, because he was the equal of any man on earth.

[illegible]

He looked eastward across the prairie. Two thousand miles away was home. The old woman would not live forever. He could afford to wait, for he was young. She could afford to be magnanimous, for he knew he was a man. He gave her the answer. "Legua," he said. "Mother."

He went home three years later. He explained no more than to say, "I lived with Crows for a while. It was some time before I could leave. They called me Horse."

He did not find it necessary either to apologize or to boast, because he was the equal of any man on earth.

The Man Who Shot Liberty Valance

Bert Barricune died in 1910. Not more than a dozen persons showed up for his funeral. Among them was an earnest young reporter who hoped for a human-interest story; there were legends that the old man had been something of a gunfighter in the early days. A few aging men tiptoed in, singly or in pairs, scowling and edgy, clutching their battered hats—men who had been Bert's companions at drinking or penny ante while the world passed them by. One woman came, wearing a heavy veil that concealed her face. White and yellow streaks showed in her black-dyed hair. The reporter made a mental note: Old friend from the old District. But no story there—can't mention that.

One by one they filed past the casket, looking into the still face of old Bert Barricune, who had been nobody. His stubbly hair was white, and his lined face was as empty in death as his life had been. But death had added dignity.

One great spray of flowers spread behind the casket. The card read, "Senator and Mrs. Ransome Foster." There were no other flowers except, almost unnoticed, a few pale, leafless, pink and yellow blossoms scattered on the carpeted step. The reporter, squinting, finally identified them: son of a gun! Blossoms of the prickly pear. Cactus flowers. Seems suitable for the old man—flowers that grow on prairie wasteland. Well, they're free if you want to pick 'em, and Barricune's friends don't look prosperous. But how come the Senator sends a bouquet?

There was a delay, and the funeral director fidgeted a little, waiting. The reporter sat up straighter when he saw the last two mourners enter.

Senator Foster—sure, there's the crippled arm—and that must be his wife. Congress is still in session; he came all the way from Washington. Why would he bother, for an old wreck like Bert Barricune?

After the funeral was decently over, the reporter asked him. The Senator almost told the truth, but he caught himself in time. He said, "Bert Barricune was my friend for more than thirty years."

He could not give the true answer: He was my enemy; he was my conscience; he made me whatever I am.

Ransome Foster had been in the Territory for seven months when he ran into Liberty Valance. He had been afoot on the prairie for two days when he met Bert Barricune. Up to that time, Ranse Foster had been nobody in particular—a dude from the East, quietly inquisitive, moving from one shack town to another; just another tenderfoot with his own reasons for being there and no aim in life at all.

When Barricune found him on the prairie, Foster

was indeed a tenderfoot. In his boots there was a warm, damp squidging where his feet had blistered, and the blisters had broken to bleed. He was bruised, sunburned, and filthy. He had been crawling, but when he saw Barricune riding toward him, he sat up. He had no horse, no saddle and, by that time, no pride.

Barricune looked down at him, not saying anything. Finally Ranse Foster asked, "Water?"

Barricune shook his head. "I don't carry none, but we can go where it is."

He stepped down from the saddle, a casual Samaritan, and with one heave pulled Foster upright.

"Git you in the saddle, can you stay there?" he inquired.

"If I can't," Foster answered through swollen lips, "shoot me."

Bert said amiably, "All right," and pulled the horse around. By twisting its ear, he held the animal quiet long enough to help the anguished stranger to the saddle. Then, on foot—and like any cowboy Bert Barricune hated walking—he led the horse five miles to the river. He let Foster lie where he fell in the cottonwood grove and brought him a hat full of water.

After that, Foster made three attempts to stand up. After the third failure, Barricune asked, grinning, "Want me to shoot you after all?"

"No," Foster answered. "There's something I want to do first."

Barricune looked at the bruises and commented,

"Well, I should think so." He got on his horse and rode away. After an hour he returned with bedding and grub and asked, "Ain't you dead yet?"

The bruised and battered man opened his uninjured eye and said, "Not yet, but soon." Bert was amused. He brought a bucket of water and set up camp—a bedroll on a tarp, an armload of wood for a fire. He crouched on his heels while the tenderfoot, with cautious movements that told of pain, got his clothes off and splashed water on his body. No gunshot wounds, Barricune observed, but marks of kicks, and a couple that must have been made with a quirt.

After a while he asked, not inquisitively, but as one who has a right to know how matters stood, "Anybody looking for you?"

Foster rubbed dust from his clothes, being too full of pain to shake them.

"No," he said. "But I'm looking for somebody."

"I ain't going to help you look," Bert informed him. "Town's over that way, two miles, when you get ready to come. Cache the stuff when you leave. I'll pick it up."

Three days later they met in the town marshal's office. They glanced at each other but did not speak. This time it was Bert Barricune who was bruised, though not much. The marshal was just letting him out of the one-cell jail when Foster limped into the office. Nobody said anything until Barricune, blinking and walking not quite steadily, had left. Foster saw him stop in front of the next building to speak to a girl.

They walked away together, and it looked as if the young man were being scolded.

The marshal cleared his throat. "You wanted something, Mister?"

Foster answered, "Three men set me afoot on the prairie. Is that an offense against the law around here?"

The marshal eased himself and his stomach into a chair and frowned judiciously. "It ain't customary," he admitted. "Who was they?"

"The boss was a big man with black hair, dark eyes, and two gold teeth in front. The other two—"

"I know. Liberty Valance and a couple of his boys. Just what's your complaint, now?" Foster began to understand that no help was going to come from the marshal.

"They rob you?" the marshal asked.

"They didn't search me."

"Take your gun?"

"I didn't have one."

"Steal your horse?"

"Gave him a crack with a quirt, and he left."

"Saddle on him?"

"No. I left it out there."

The marshal shook his head. "Can't see you got any legal complaint," he said with relief. "Where was this?"

"On a road in the woods, by a creek. Two days' walk from here."

The marshal got to his feet. "You don't even know

what jurisdiction it was in. They knocked you around; well, that could happen. Man gets in a fight—could happen to anybody."

Foster said dryly, "Thanks a lot."

The marshal stopped him as he reached the door. "There's a reward for Liberty Valance."

"I still haven't got a gun," Foster said. "Does he come here often?"

"Nope. Nothing he'd want in Twotrees. Hard man to find." The marshal looked Foster up and down. "He won't come after you here." It was as if he had added, *Sonny!* "Beat you up once, he won't come again for that."

And I, Foster realized, am not man enough to go after him.

"Fact is," the marshal added, "I can't think of any bait that would bring him in. Pretty quiet here. Yes sir." He put his thumbs in his galluses and looked out the window, taking credit for the quietness.

Bait, Foster thought. He went out thinking about it. For the first time in a couple of years he had an ambition—not a laudable one, but something to aim at. He was going to be the bait for Liberty Valance and, as far as he could be, the trap as well.

At the Elite Cafe he stood meekly in the doorway, hat in hand, like a man who expects and deserves to be refused anything he might ask for. Clearing his throat, he asked, "Could I work for a meal?"

The girl who was filling sugar bowls looked up and pitied him. "Why, I should think so. Mr. Anderson!"

She was the girl who had walked away with Barricune, scolding him.

The proprietor came from the kitchen, and Ranse Foster repeated his question, cringing, but with a suggestion of a sneer.

"Go around back and split some wood," Anderson answered, turning back to the kitchen.

"He could just as well eat first," the waitress suggested. "I'll dish up some stew to begin with."

Ranse ate fast, as if he expected the plate to be snatched away. He knew the girl glanced at him several times, and he hated her for it. He had not counted on anyone's pitying him in his new role of sneering humility, but he knew he might as well get used to it.

When she brought his pie, she said, "If you was looking for a job . . ."

He forced himself to look at her suspiciously. "Yes?"

"You could try the Prairie Belle. I heard they needed a swamper."

Bert Barricune, riding out to the river camp for his bedroll, hardly knew the man he met there. Ranse Foster was haughty, condescending, and cringing all at once. He spoke with a faint sneer, and stood as if he expected to be kicked.

"I assumed you'd be back for your belongings," he said. "I realized that you would change your mind."

Barricune, strapping up his bedroll, looked blank. "Never changed it," he disagreed. "Doing just what I planned. I never give you my bedroll."

"Of course not, of course not," the new Ranse Foster agreed with sneering humility. "It's yours. You have every right to reclaim it."

Barricune looked at him narrowly and hoisted the bedroll to sling it up behind his saddle. "I should have left you for the buzzards," he remarked.

Foster agreed, with a smile that should have got him a fist in the teeth. "Thank you, my friend," he said with no gratitude. "Thank you for all your kindness, which I have done nothing to deserve and shall do nothing to repay."

Barricune rode off, scowling, with the memory of his good deed irritating him like lice. The new Foster followed, far behind, on foot.

Sometimes in later life Ranse Foster thought of the several men he had been through the years. He did not admire any of them very much. He was by no means ashamed of the man he finally became, except that he owed too much to other people. One man he had been when he was young, a serious student, gullible and quick-tempered. Another man had been reckless and without an aim; he went West, with two thousand dollars of his own, after a quarrel with the executor of his father's estate. That man did not last long. Liberty Valance had whipped him with a quirt and kicked him into unconsciousness, for no reason except that Liberty, meeting him and knowing him for a tenderfoot, was able to do so. That man died on the prairie. After that, there was the man who set out to be the bait that would bring Liberty Valance into Twotrees.

Ranse Foster had never hated anyone before he met Liberty Valance, but Liberty was not the last man he learned to hate. He hated the man he himself had been while he waited to meet Liberty again.

The swamper's job at the Prairie Belle was not disgraceful until Ranse Foster made it so. When he swept floors, he was so obviously contemptuous of the work and of himself for doing it that other men saw him as contemptible. He watched the customers with a curled lip as if they were beneath him. But when a poker player threw a white chip on the floor, the swamper looked at him with half-veiled hatred—and picked up the chip. They talked about him at the Prairie Belle, because he could not be ignored.

At the end of the first month, he bought a Colt .45 from a drunken cowboy who needed money worse than he needed two guns. After that, Ranse went without part of his sleep in order to walk out, seven mornings a week, to where his first camp had been and practice target shooting. And the second time he overslept from exhaustion, Joe Mosten of the Prairie Belle fired him.

"Here's your pay," Joe growled, and dropped the money on the floor.

A week passed before he got another job. He ate his meals frugally in the Elite Cafe and let himself be seen stealing scraps off plates that other diners had left. Lillian, the older of the two waitresses, yelled her disgust, but Hallie, who was young, pitied him.

"Come to the back door when it's dark," she murmured, "and I'll give you a bite. There's plenty to spare."

The second evening he went to the back door, Bert Barricune was there ahead of him. He said gently, "Hallie is my girl."

"No offense intended," Foster answered. "The young lady offered me food, and I have come to get it."

"A dog eats where it can," young Barricune drawled.

Ranse's muscles tensed and rage mounted in his throat, but he caught himself in time and shrugged. Bert said something then that scared him: "If you wanted to get talked about, it's working fine. They're talking clean over in Dunbar."

"What they do or say in Dunbar," Foster answered, "is nothing to me."

"It's where Liberty Valance hangs out," the other man said casually. "In case you care."

Ranse almost confided then, but instead said stiffly, "I do not quite appreciate your strange interest in my affairs."

Barricune pushed back his hat and scratched his head. "I don't understand it myself. But leave my girl alone."

"As charming as Miss Hallie may be," Ranse told him, "I am interested only in keeping my stomach filled."

"Then why don't you work for a living? The clerk at Dowitt's quit this afternoon."

Jake Dowitt hired him as a clerk because nobody else wanted the job.

"Read and write, do you?" Dowitt asked. "Work with figures?"

Foster drew himself up. "Sir, whatever may be said against me, I believe I may lay claim to being a scholar. That much I claim, if nothing more. I have read law."

"Maybe the job ain't good enough for you," Dowitt suggested.

Foster became humble again. "Any job is good enough for me. I will also sweep the floor."

"You will also keep up the fire in the stove," Dowitt told him. "Seven in the morning till nine at night. Got a place to live?"

"I sleep in the livery stable in return for keeping it shoveled out."

Dowitt had intended to house his clerk in a small room over the store, but he changed his mind. "Got a shed out back you can bunk in," he offered. "You'll have to clean it out first. Used to keep chickens there."

"There is one thing," Foster said. "I want two half-days off a week."

Dowitt looked over the top of his spectacles. "Now what would you do with time off? Never mind. You can have it—for less pay. I give you a discount on what you buy in the store."

The only purchase Foster made consisted of four boxes of cartridges a week.

In the store, he weighed salt pork as if it were low stuff but himself still lower, humbly measured lengths of dress goods for the women customers. He added vanity to his other unpleasantnesses and let customers discover him combing his hair admiringly before a small mirror. He let himself be seen reading a small black book, which aroused curiosity.

It was while he worked at the store that he started Twotrees' first school. Hallie was responsible for that. Handing him a plate heaped higher than other customers got at the cafe, she said gently, "You're a learned man, they say, Mr. Foster."

With Hallie he could no longer sneer or pretend humility, for Hallie was herself humble, as well as gentle and kind. He protected himself from her by not speaking unless he had to.

He answered, "I have had advantages, Miss Hallie, before fate brought me here."

"That book you read," she asked wistfully, "what's it about?"

"It was written by a man named Plato," Ranse told her stiffly. "It was written in Greek."

She brought him a cup of coffee, hesitated for a moment, and then asked, "You can read and write American, too, can't you?"

"English, Miss Hallie," he corrected. "English is our mother tongue. I am quite familiar with English."

She put her red hands on the cafe counter. "Mr. Foster," she whispered, "will you teach me to read?"

He was too startled to think of an answer she could not defeat.

"Bert wouldn't like it," he said. "You're a grown woman besides. It wouldn't look right for you to be learning to read now."

She shook her head. "I can't learn any younger." She sighed. "I always wanted to know how to read and write." She walked away toward the kitchen, and Ranse Foster was struck with an emotion he knew he could not afford. He was swept with pity. He called her back.

"Miss Hallie. Not you alone—people would talk about you. But if you brought Bert—"

"Bert can already read some. He don't care about it. But there's some kids in town." Her face was so lighted that Ranse looked away.

He still tried to escape. "Won't you be ashamed, learning with children?"

"Why, I'll be proud to learn any way at all," she said.

He had three little girls, two restless little boys, and Hallie in Twotrees' first school sessions—one hour each afternoon, in Dowitt's storeroom. Dowitt did not dock his pay for the time spent, but he puzzled a great deal. So did the children's parents. The children themselves were puzzled at some of the things he read aloud, but they were patient. After all, lessons lasted only an hour.

"When you are older, you will understand this," he promised, not looking at Hallie, and then he read

Shakespeare's sonnet that begins:

No longer mourn for me when I am dead
Than you shall hear the surly sullen bell

and ends:

Do not so much as my poor name rehearse,
But let your love even with my life decay,
Lest the wise world should look into your moan
And mock you with me after I am gone.

Hallie understood the warning, he knew. He read another sonnet, too:

When in disgrace with Fortune and men's eyes,
I all alone beweep my outcast state,

and carefully did not look up at her as he finished it:

For thy sweet love rememb'red such wealth brings
That then I scorn to change my state with kings.

Her earnestness in learning was distasteful to him—the anxious way she grasped a pencil and formed letters, the little gasp with which she always began to read aloud. Twice he made her cry, but she never missed a lesson.

He wished he had a teacher for his own learning, but

he could not trust anyone, and so he did his lessons alone. Bert Barricune caught him at it on one of those free afternoons when Foster, on a horse from the livery stable, had ridden miles out of town to a secluded spot.

Ranse Foster had an empty gun in his hand when Barricune stepped out from behind a sandstone column and remarked, "I've seen better."

Foster whirled, and Barricune added, "I could have been somebody else—and your gun's empty."

"When I see somebody else, it won't be," Foster promised.

"If you'd asked me," Barricune mused, "I could've helped you. But you didn't want no helping. A man shouldn't be ashamed to ask somebody that knows better than him." His gun was suddenly in his hand, and five shots cracked their echoes around the skull-white sandstone pillars. Half an inch above each of five cards that Ranse had tacked to a dead tree, at the level of a man's waist, a splintered hole appeared in the wood. "Didn't want to spoil your targets," Barricune explained.

"I'm not ashamed to ask you," Foster told him angrily, "since you know so much. I shoot straight but slow. I'm asking you now."

Barricune, reloading his gun, shook his head. "It's kind of late for that. I come out to tell you that Liberty Valance is in town. He's interested in the dude that anybody can kick around—this here tenderfoot that boasts how he can read Greek."

"Well," said Foster softly. "Well, so the time has come."

"Don't figure you're riding into town with me," Bert warned. "You're coming all by yourself."

Ranse rode into town with his gun belt buckled on. Always before, he had carried it wrapped in a slicker. In town, he allowed himself the luxury of one last vanity. He went to the barbershop, neither sneering nor cringing, and said sharply, "Cut my hair. Short."

The barber was nervous, but he worked understandably fast.

"Thought you was partial to that long wavy hair of yourn," he remarked.

"I don't know why you thought so," Foster said coldly.

Out in the street again, he realized that he did not know how to go about the job. He did not know where Liberty Valance was, and he was determined not to be caught like a rat. He intended to look for Liberty.

Joe Mosten's right-hand man was lounging at the door of the Prairie Belle. He moved over to bar the way.

"Not in there, Foster," he said gently. It was the first time in months that Ranse Foster had heard another man address him respectfully. His presence was recognized—as a menace to the fixtures of the Prairie Belle.

When I die, sometime today, he thought, they won't say I was a coward. They may say I was a damn fool, but I won't care by that time.

"Where is he?" Ranse asked.

"I couldn't tell you that," the man said apologetically. "I'm young and healthy, and where he is is none of my business. Joe'd be obliged if you stay out of the bar, that's all."

Ranse looked across toward Dowitt's store. The padlock was on the door. He glanced north, toward the marshal's office.

"That's closed, too," the saloon man told him courteously. "Marshal was called out of town an hour ago."

Ranse threw back his head and laughed. The sound echoed back from the false-fronted buildings across the street. There was nobody walking in the street; there were not even any horses tied to the hitching racks.

"Send Liberty word," he ordered in the tone of one who has a right to command. "Tell him the tenderfoot wants to see him again."

The saloon man cleared his throat. "Guess it won't be necessary. That's him coming down at the end of the street, wouldn't you say?"

Ranse looked, knowing the saloon man was watching him curiously.

"I'd say it is," he agreed. "Yes, I'd say that was Liberty Valance."

"I'll be going inside now," the other man remarked apologetically. "Well, take care of yourself." He was gone without a sound.

This is the classic situation, Ranse realized. Two

enemies walking to meet each other along the dusty, waiting street of a western town. What reasons other men have had, I will never know. There are so many things I have never learned! And now there is no time left.

He was an actor who knew the end of the scene but had forgotten the lines and never knew the cue for them. Onc of us ought to say something, he realized. I should have planned this all out in advance. But all I ever saw was the end of it.

Liberty Valance, burly and broad-shouldered, walked stiff-legged, with his elbows bent.

When he is close enough for me to see whether he is smiling, Ranse Foster thought, somebody's got to speak.

He looked into his own mind and realized, This man is afraid, this Ransome Foster. But nobody else knows it. He walks and is afraid, but he is no coward. Let them remember that. Let Hallie remember that.

Liberty Valance gave the cue. "Looking for me?" he called between his teeth. He was grinning.

Ranse was almost grateful to him; it was as if Liberty had said, The time is now!

"I owe you something," Ranse answered. "I want to pay my debt."

Liberty's hand flashed with his own. The gun in Foster's hand exploded, and so did the whole world.

Two shots to my one, he thought—his last thought for a while.

He looked up at a strange, unsteady ceiling and a

face that wavered like a reflection in water. The bed beneath him swung even after he closed his eyes. Far away someone said, "Shove some more cloth in the wound. It slows the bleeding."

He knew with certain agony where the wound was—in his right shoulder. When they touched it, he heard himself cry out.

The face that wavered above him was a new one, Bert Barricune's.

"He's dead," Barricune said.

Foster answered from far away, "I am not."

Barricune said, "I didn't mean you."

Ranse turned his head away from the pain, and the face that had shivered above him before was Hallie's, white and big-eyed. She put a hesitant hand on his, and he was annoyed to see that hers was trembling.

"Are you shaking," he asked, "because there's blood on my hands?"

"No," she answered. "It's because they might have been getting cold."

He was aware then that other people were in the room; they stirred and moved aside as the doctor entered.

"Maybe you're gonna keep that arm," the doctor told him at last. "But it's never gonna be much use to you."

The trial was held three weeks after the shooting, in the hotel room where Ranse lay in bed. The charge was disturbing the peace; he pleaded guilty and was fined ten dollars.

When the others had gone, he told Bert Barricune, "There was a reward, I heard. That would pay the doctor and the hotel."

"You ain't going to collect it," Bert informed him. "It'd make you too big for your britches." Barricune sat looking at him for a moment and then remarked, "You didn't kill Liberty."

Foster frowned. "They buried him."

"Liberty fired once. You fired once and missed. I fired once, and I don't generally miss. I ain't going to collect the reward, neither. Hallie don't hold with violence."

Foster said thoughtfully, "That was all I had to be proud of."

"You faced him," Barricune said. "You went to meet him. If you got to be proud of something, you can remember that. It's a fact you ain't got much else."

Ranse looked at him with narrowed eyes. "Bert, are you a friend of mine?"

Bert smiled without humor. "You know I ain't. I picked you up off the prairie, but I'd do that for the lowest scum that crawls. I wisht I hadn't."

"Then why—"

Bert looked at the toe of his boot. "Hallie likes you. I'm a friend of Hallie's. That's all I ever will be, long as you're around."

Ranse said, "Then I shot Liberty Valance." That was the nearest he ever dared come to saying "Thank you." And that was when Bert Barricune started being his conscience, his Nemesis, his lifelong enemy and the man who made him great.

"Would she be happy living back East?" Foster asked. "There's money waiting for me there if I go back."

Bert answered. "What do you think?" He stood up and stretched. "You got quite a problem, ain't you? You could solve it easy by just going back alone. There ain't much a man can do here with a crippled arm."

He went out and shut the door behind him.

There is always a way out, Foster thought, if a man wants to take it. Bert had been his way out when he met Liberty on the street of Twotrees. To go home was the way out of this.

I learned to live without pride, he told himself. I could learn to forget about Hallie.

When she came, between the dinner dishes and setting the tables for supper at the cafe, he told her.

She did not cry. Sitting in the chair beside his bed, she winced and jerked one hand in protest when he said, "As soon as I can travel, I'll be going back where I came from."

She did not argue. She said only, "I wish you good luck, Ransome. Bert and me, we'll look after you long as you stay. And remember you after you're gone."

"How will you remember me?" he demanded harshly.

As his student she had been humble, but as a woman she had her pride. "Don't ask that," she said, and got up from the chair.

"Hallie, Hallie," he pleaded, "how can I stay? How can I earn a living?"

She said indignantly, as if someone else had insulted him, "Ranse Foster, I just guess you could do anything you wanted to."

"Hallie," he said gently, "sit down."

He never really wanted to be outstanding. He had two aims in life: to make Hallie happy and to keep Bert Barricune out of trouble. He defended Bert on charges ranging from drunkenness to stealing cattle, and Bert served time twice.

Ranse Foster did not want to run for judge, but Bert remarked, "I think Hallie would kind of like it if you was His Honor." Hallie was pleased but not surprised when he was elected. Ranse was surprised but not pleased.

He was not eager to run for the legislature—that was after the territory became a state—but there was Bert Barricune in the background, never urging, never advising, but watching with half-closed, bloodshot eyes. Bert Barricune, who never amounted to anything, but never intruded, was a living, silent reminder of three debts: a hat full of water under the cottonwoods, gunfire in a dusty street, and Hallie, quietly sewing beside a lamp in the parlor. And the Fosters had four sons.

All the things the opposition said about Ranse Foster when he ran for the state legislature were true, except one. He had been a lowly swamper in a frontier saloon; he had been a dead beat, accepting handouts at the alley entrance of a cafe; he had been despicable and despised. But the accusation that lost him the election was false. He had not killed Liberty Valance. He never served in the state legislature.

When there was talk of his running for governor, he refused. Handy Strong, who knew politics, tried to persuade him.

"That shooting, we'll get around that. 'The Honorable Ransome Foster walked down a street in broad daylight to meet an enemy of society. He shot him down in a fair fight, of necessity, the way you'd shoot a mad dog—but Liberty Valance could shoot back, and he did. Ranse Foster carries the mark of that encounter today in a crippled right arm. He is still paying the price for protecting law-abiding citizens. And he was the first teacher west of Rosy Buttes. He served without pay.' You've come a long way, Ranse, and you're going further."

"A long way," Foster agreed, "for a man who never wanted to go anywhere. I don't want to be governor."

When Handy had gone, Bert Barricune sagged in, unwashed, unshaven. He sat down stiffly. At the age of fifty, he was an old man, an unwanted relic of the frontier that was gone, a legacy to more civilized times that had no place for him. He filled his pipe deliberately. After a while he remarked, "The other side is gonna say you ain't fitten to be governor. Because your wife ain't fancy enough. They're gonna say Hallie didn't even learn to read till she was growed up."

Ranse was on his feet, white with fury. "Then I'm going to win this election if it kills me."

"I don't reckon it'll kill you," Bert drawled. "Liberty Valance couldn't."

"I could have got rid of the weight of that affair long ago," Ranse reminded him, "by telling the truth."

"You could yet," Bert answered. "Why don't you?"

Ranse said bitterly, "Because I owe you too much . . . I don't think Hallie wants to be the governor's lady. She's shy."

"Hallie don't never want nothing for herself. She wants things for you. The way I feel, I wouldn't mourn at your funeral. But what Hallie wants, I'm gonna try to see she gets."

"So am I," Ranse promised grimly.

"Then I don't mind telling you," Bert admitted, "that it was me reminded the opposition to dig up that matter of how she couldn't read."

As the Senator and his wife rode out to the airport after old Bert Barricune's barren funeral, Hallie sighed. "Bert never had much of anything. I guess he never wanted much."

He wanted you to be happy, Ranse Foster thought, and he did the best he knew how.

"I wonder where those prickly-pear blossoms came from," he mused.

Hallie glanced up at him, smiling. "From me," she said.

Lost Sister

Our household was full of women, who overwhelmed my Uncle Charlie and sometimes confused me with their bustle and chatter. We were the only men on the place. I was nine years old when still another woman came—Aunt Bessie, who had been living with the Indians.

When my mother told me about her, I couldn't believe it. The savages had killed my father, a cavalry lieutenant, two years before. I hated Indians and looked forward to wiping them out when I got older. (But when I was grown, they were no menace any more.)

"What did she live with the hostiles for?" I demanded.

"They captured her when she was a little girl," Ma said. "She was three years younger than you are. Now she's coming home."

High time she came home, I thought. I said so, promising, "If they was ever to get me, I wouldn't stay with 'em long."

Ma put her arms around me. "Don't talk like that. They won't get you. They'll never get you."

I was my mother's only real tie with her husband's family. She was not happy with those masterful women, my Aunts Margaret, Hannah and Sabina, but she would not go back East where she came from. Uncle Charlie managed the store the aunts owned, but he wasn't really a member of the family—he was just Aunt Margaret's husband. The only man who had belonged was my father, the aunts' younger brother. And I belonged, and someday the store would be mine. My mother stayed to protect my heritage.

None of the three sisters, my aunts, had ever seen Aunt Bessie. She had been taken by the Indians before they were born. Aunt Mary had known her—Aunt Mary was two years older—but she lived a thousand miles away now and was not well.

There was no picture of the little girl who had become a legend. When the family had first settled here, there was enough struggle to feed and clothe the children without having pictures made of them.

Even after Army officers had come to our house several times and there had been many letters about Aunt Bessie's delivery from the savages, it was a long time before she came. Major Harris, who made the final arrangements, warned my aunts that they would have problems, that Aunt Bessie might not be able to settle down easily into family life.

This was only a challenge to Aunt Margaret, who welcomed challenges. "She's our own flesh and blood," Aunt Margaret trumpeted. "Of course she must come to us. My poor, dear sister Bessie, torn from her home forty years ago!"

The major was earnest but not tactful. "She's been with the savages all those years," he insisted. "And she was only a little girl when she was taken. I haven't seen her myself, but it's reasonable to assume that she'll be like an Indian woman."

My stately Aunt Margaret arose to show that the audience was ended. "Major Harris," she intoned, "I cannot permit anyone to criticize my own dear sister. She will live in my home, and if I do not receive official word that she is coming within a month, I shall take steps."

Aunt Bessie came before the month was up.

The aunts in residence made valiant preparations. They bustled and swept and mopped and polished. They moved me from my own room to my mother's—as she had been begging them to do because I was troubled with nightmares. They prepared my old room for Aunt Bessie with many small comforts—fresh doilies everywhere, hairpins, a matching pitcher and bowl, the best towels and two new nightgowns in case hers might be old. (The fact was that she didn't have any.)

"Perhaps we should have some dresses made," Hannah suggested. "We don't know what she'll have with her."

"We don't know what size she'll take, either," Margaret pointed out. "There'll be time enough for her to go to the store after she settles down and rests for a day or two. Then she can shop to her heart's content."

Ladies of the town came to call almost every afternoon while the preparations were going on. Margaret promised then that, as soon as Bessie had recovered sufficiently from her ordeal, they should all meet her at tea.

Margaret warned her anxious sisters, "Now, girls, we mustn't ask her too many questions at first. She must rest for a while. She's been through a terrible experience." Margaret's voice dropped way down with those last two words, as if only she could be expected to understand.

Indeed Bessie had been through a terrible experience, but it wasn't what the sisters thought. The experience from which she was suffering, when she arrived, was that she had been wrenched from her people, the Indians, and turned over to strangers. She had not been freed. She had been made a captive.

Aunt Bessie came with Major Harris and an interpreter, a half-blood with greasy black hair hanging down to his shoulders. His costume was half Army and half primitive. Aunt Margaret swung the door open wide when she saw them coming. She ran out with her sisters following, while my mother and I watched from a window. Margaret's arms were outstretched, but when she saw the woman closer, her arms dropped and her glad cry died.

She did not cringe, my Aunt Bessie who had been an Indian for forty years, but she stopped walking and stood staring, helpless among her captors.

The sisters had described her often as a little girl. Not that they had ever seen her, but she was a legend, the captive child. Beautiful blonde curls, they said she had, and big blue eyes—she was a fairy child, a pale-haired little angel who ran on dancing feet.

The Bessie who came back was an aging woman who plodded in moccasins, whose dark dress did not belong on her bulging body. Her brown hair hung just below her ears. It was growing out; when she was first taken from the Indians, her hair had been cut short to clean out the vermin.

Aunt Margaret recovered herself and, instead of embracing this silent stolid woman, satisfied herself by patting an arm and crying, "Poor dear Bessie, I am your sister Margaret. And here are our sisters Hannah and Sabina. We do hope you're not all tired out from your journey!"

Aunt Margaret was all graciousness, because she had been assured beyond doubt that this was truly a member of the family. She must have believed—Aunt Margaret could believe anything—that all Bessie needed was to have a nice nap and wash her face. Then she would be as talkative as any of them.

The other aunts were quick-moving and sharp of tongue. But this one moved as if her sorrows were a burden on her bowed shoulders, and when she spoke briefly in answer to the interpreter, you could not understand a word of it.

Aunt Margaret ignored these peculiarities. She took the party into the front parlor—even the interpreter, when she understood there was no avoiding it. She might have gone on battling with the Major about him, but she was in a hurry to talk to her lost sister.

"You won't be able to converse with her unless the

interpreter is present," Major Harris said. "Not," he explained hastily, "because of any regulation, but because she has forgotten English."

Aunt Margaret gave the half-blood interpreter a look of frowning doubt and let him enter. She coaxed Bessie. "Come, dear, sit down."

The interpreter mumbled, and my Indian aunt sat cautiously on a needlepoint chair. For most of her life she had been living with people who sat comfortably on the ground.

The visit in the parlor was brief. Bessie had had her instructions before she came. But Major Harris had a few warnings for the family. "Technically, your sister is still a prisoner," he explained, ignoring Margaret's start of horror. "She will be in your custody. She may walk in your fenced yard, but she must not leave it without official permission.

"Mrs. Raleigh, this may be a heavy burden for you all. But she has been told all this and has expressed willingness to conform to these restrictions. I don't think you will have any trouble keeping her here." Major Harris hesitated, remembered that he was a soldier and a brave man, and added, "If I did, I wouldn't have brought her."

There was the making of a sharp little battle, but Aunt Margaret chose to overlook the challenge. She could not overlook the fact that Bessie was not what she had expected.

Bessie certainly knew that this was her lost white family, but she didn't seem to care. She was infinitely sad, infinitely removed. She asked one question: "Mary?" and Aunt Margaret almost wept with joy.

"Sister Mary lives a long way from here," she explained, "and she isn't well, but she will come as soon as she's able. Dear sister Mary!"

The interpreter translated this, and Bessie had no more to say. That was the only understandable word she ever did say in our house, the remembered name of her older sister.

When the aunts, all chattering, took Bessie to her room, one of them asked, "But where are her things?"

Bessie had no things, no baggage. She had nothing at all but the clothes she stood in. While the sisters scurried to bring a comb and other oddments, she stood like a stooped monument, silent and watchful. This was her prison. Very well, she would endure it.

"Maybe tomorrow we can take her to the store and see what she would like," Aunt Hannah suggested.

"There's no hurry," Aunt Margaret declared thoughtfully. She was getting the idea that this sister was going to be a problem. But I don't think Aunt Margaret ever really stopped hoping that one day Bessie would cease to be different, that she would end her stubborn silence and begin to relate the events of her life among the savages, in the parlor over a cup of tea.

My Indian aunt accustomed herself, finally, to sitting on the chair in her room. She seldom came out, which was a relief to her sisters. She preferred to stand, hour after hour, looking out the window—which was open only about a foot, in spite of all Uncle

Charlie's efforts to budge it higher. And she always wore moccasins. She was never able to wear shoes from the store, but seemed to treasure the shoes brought to her.

The aunts did not, of course, take her shopping after all. They made her a couple of dresses; and when they told her, with signs and voluble explanations, to change her dress, she did.

After I found that she was usually at the window, looking across the flat land to the blue mountains, I played in the yard so I could stare at her. She never smiled, as an aunt should, but she looked at me sometimes, thoughtfully, as if measuring my worth. By performing athletic feats, such as walking on my hands, I could get her attention. For some reason, I valued it.

She didn't often change expression, but twice I saw her scowl with disapproval. Once was when one of the aunts slapped me in a casual way. I had earned the slap, but the Indians did not punish children with blows. Aunt Bessie was shocked, I think, to see that white people did. The other time was when I talked back to someone with spoiled, small-boy insolence—and that time the scowl was for me.

The sisters and my mother took turns, as was their Christian duty, in visiting her for half an hour each day. Bessie didn't eat at the table with us—not after the first meal.

The first time my mother took her turn, it was under protest. "I'm afraid I'd start crying in front of her," she argued, but Aunt Margaret insisted.

I was lurking in the hall when Ma went in. Bessie said something, then said it again, peremptorily, until my mother guessed what she wanted. She called me and put her arm around me as I stood beside her chair. Aunt Bessie nodded, and that was all there was to it.

Afterward, my mother said, "She likes you. And so do I." She kissed me.

"I don't like her," I complained. "She's queer."

"She's a sad old lady," my mother explained. "She had a little boy once, you know."

"What happened to him?"

"He grew up and became a warrior. I suppose she was proud of him. Now the Army has him in prison somewhere. He's half Indian. He was a dangerous man."

He was indeed a dangerous man, and a proud man, a chief, a bird of prey whose wings the Army had clipped after bitter years of trying.

However, my mother and my Indian aunt had that one thing in common: they both had sons. The other aunts were childless.

There was a great to-do about having Aunt Bessie's photograph taken. The aunts who were stubbornly and valiantly trying to make her one of the family wanted a picture of her for the family album. The government wanted one too, for some reason—perhaps because someone realized that a thing of historic importance had been accomplished by recovering the captive child.

Major Harris sent a young lieutenant with the

greasy-haired interpreter to discuss the matter in the parlor. (Margaret, with great foresight, put a clean towel on a chair and saw to it the interpreter sat there.) Bessie spoke very little during that meeting, and of course we understood only what the half-blood *said* she was saying.

No, she did not want her picture made. No.

But your son had his picture made. Do you want to see it? They teased her with that offer, and she nodded.

If we let you see his picture, then will you have yours made?

She nodded doubtfully. Then she demanded more than had been offered: If you let me keep his picture, then you can make mine.

No, you can only look at it. We have to keep his picture. It belongs to us.

My Indian aunt gambled for high stakes. She shrugged and spoke, and the interpreter said, "She not want to look. She will keep or nothing."

My mother shivered, understanding as the aunts could not understand what Bessie was gambling—all or nothing.

Bessie won. Perhaps they had intended that she should. She was allowed to keep the photograph that had been made of her son. It has been in history books many times—the half-white chief, the valiant leader who was not quite great enough to keep his Indian people free.

His photograph was taken after he was captured, but you would never guess it. His head is high, his eyes stare with boldness but not with scorn, his long hair is arranged with care—dark hair braided on one side and with a tendency to curl where the other side hangs loose—and his hands hold the pipe like a royal scepter.

That photograph of the captive but unconquered warrior had its effect on me. Remembering him, I began to control my temper and my tongue, to cultivate reserve as I grew older, to stare with boldness but not scorn at people who annoyed or offended me. I never met him, but I took silent pride in him—Eagle Head, my Indian cousin.

Bessie kept his picture on her dresser when she was not holding it in her hands. And she went like a docile, silent child to the photograph studio, in a carriage with Aunt Margaret early one morning, when there would be few people on the street to stare.

Bessie's photograph is not proud but pitiful. She looks out with no expression. There is no emotion there, no challenge, only the face of an aging woman with short hair, only endurance and patience. The aunts put a copy in the family album.

But they were nearing the end of their tether. The Indian aunt was a solid ghost in the house. She did nothing because there was nothing for her to do. Her gnarled hands must have been skilled at squaws' work, at butchering meat and scraping and tanning hides, at making teepees and beading ceremonial clothes. But her skills were useless and unwanted in a civilized home. She did not even sew when my mother gave her cloth and needles and thread. She kept the sewing things beside her son's picture.

She ate (in her room) and slept (on the floor) and stood looking out the window. That was all, and it could not go on. But it had to go on, at least until my sick Aunt Mary was well enough to travel—Aunt Mary who was her older sister, the only one who had known her when they were children.

The sisters' duty visits to Aunt Bessie became less and less visits and more and more duty. They settled into a bearable routine. Margaret had taken upon herself the responsibility of trying to make Bessie talk. Make, I said, not teach. She firmly believed that her stubborn and unfortunate sister needed only encouragement from a strong-willed person. So Margaret talked, as to a child, when she bustled in:

"Now there you stand, just looking, dear. What in the world is there to see out there? The birds—are you watching the birds? Why don't you try sewing? Or you could go for a little walk in the yard. Don't you want to go out for a nice little walk?"

Bessie listened and blinked.

Margaret could have understood an Indian woman's not being able to converse in a civilized tongue, but her own sister was not an Indian. Bessie was white, therefore she should talk the language her sisters did—the language she had not heard since early childhood.

Hannah, the put-upon aunt, talked to Bessie too, but she was delighted not to get any answers and not to be interrupted. She bent over her embroidery when it was her turn to sit with Bessie and told her troubles in an unending flow. Bessie stood looking out the window the whole time.

Sabina, who had just as many troubles, most of them emanating from Margaret and Hannah, went in like a martyr, firmly clutching her Bible, and read aloud from it until her time was up. She took a small clock along so that she would not, because of annoyance, be tempted to cheat.

After several weeks Aunt Mary came, white and trembling and exhausted from her illness and the long, hard journey. The sisters tried to get the interpreter in but were not successful. (Aunt Margaret took that failure pretty hard.) They briefed Aunt Mary, after she had rested, so the shock of seeing Bessie, would not be too terrible. I saw them meet, those two.

Margaret went to the Indian woman's door and explained volubly who had come, a useless but brave attempt. Then she stood aside, and Aunt Mary was there, her lined white face aglow, her arms outstretched. "Bessie! Sister Bessie!" she cried.

And after one brief moment's hesitation, Bessie went into her arms and Mary kissed her sun-dark, weathered cheek. Bessie spoke. "Ma-ry," she said. "Ma-ry." She stood with tears running down her face and her mouth working. So much to tell, so much suffering and fear—and joy and triumph, too—and the sister there at last who might legitimately hear it all and understand.

But the only English word that Bessie remembered was "Mary," and she had not cared to learn any others. She turned to the dresser, took her son's picture in her work-hardened hands, reverently, and held it so her sister could see. Her eyes pleaded.

Mary looked on the calm, noble, savage face of her half-blood nephew and said the right thing: "My, isn't he handsome!" She put her head on one side and then the other. "A fine boy, sister," she approved. "You must" she stopped, but she finished—"be awfully proud of him, dear!"

Bessie understood the tone if not the words. The tone was admiration. Her son was accepted by the sister who mattered. Bessie looked at the picture and nodded, murmuring. Then she put it back on the dresser.

Aunt Mary did not try to make Bessie talk. She sat with her every day for hours and Bessie did talk—but not in English. They sat holding hands for mutual comfort while the captive child, grown old and a grandmother, told what had happened in forty years. Aunt Mary said that was what Bessie was talking about. But she didn't understand a word of it and didn't need to.

"There is time enough for her to learn English again," Aunt Mary said. "I think she understands more than she lets on. I asked her if she'd like to come and live with me, and she nodded. We'll have the rest of our lives for her to learn English. But what she has been telling me—she can't wait to tell that.

About her life, and her son."

"Are you sure, Mary dear, that you should take the responsibility of having her?" Margaret asked dutifully, no doubt shaking in her shoes for fear Mary would change her mind now that deliverance was in sight. "I do believe she'd be happier with you, though we've done all we could."

Margaret and the other sisters would certainly be happier with Bessie somewhere else. And so, it developed, would the United States government.

Major Harris came with the interpreter to discuss details, and they told Bessie she could go, if she wished, to live with Mary a thousand miles away. Bessie was patient and willing, stolidly agreeable. She talked a great deal more to the interpreter than she had ever done before. He answered at length and then explained to the others that she wanted to know how she and Mary would travel to this far country. It was hard, he said, for her to understand just how far they were going.

Later we knew that the interpreter and Bessie had talked about much more than that.

Next morning, when Sabina took breakfast to Bessie's room, we heard a cry of dismay. Sabina stood holding the tray, repeating, "She's gone out the window! She's gone out the window!"

And so she had. The window that had always stuck so that it would not raise more than a foot was open wider now. And the photograph of Bessie's son was gone from the dresser. Nothing else was missing except Bessie and the decent dark dress she had worn the day before.

My Uncle Charlie got no breakfast that morning. With Margaret shrieking orders, he leaped on a horse and rode to the telegraph station.

Before Major Harris got there with half a dozen cavalrymen, civilian scouts were out searching for the missing woman. They were expert trackers. Their lives had depended, at various times, on their ability to read the meaning of a turned stone, a broken twig, a bruised leaf. They found that Bessie had gone south. They tracked her for ten miles. And then they lost the trail, for Bessie was as skilled as they were. Her life had sometimes depended on leaving no stone or twig or leaf marked by her passage. She traveled fast at first. Then, with time to be careful, she evaded the followers she knew would come.

The aunts were stricken with grief—at least Aunt Mary was—and bowed with humiliation about what Bessie had done. The blinds were drawn, and voices were low in the house. We had been pitied because of Bessie's tragic folly in having let the Indians make a savage of her. But now we were traitors because we had let her get away.

Aunt Mary kept saying pitifully, "Oh, why did she go? I thought she would be contented with me!"

The others said that it was, perhaps, all for the best.

Aunt Margaret proclaimed, "She has gone back to her own." That was what they honestly believed, and so did Major Harris.

My mother told me why she had gone. "You know that picture she had of the Indian chief, her son? He's escaped from the jail he was in. The fort got word of it and they think Bessie may be going to where he's hiding. That's why they're trying so hard to find her. They think," my mother explained, "that she knew of his escape before they did. They think the interpreter told her when he was here. There was no other way she could have found out."

They scoured the mountains to the south for Eagle Head and Bessie. They never found her, and they did not get him until a year later, far to the north. They could not capture him that time. He died fighting.

After I grew up, I operated the family store, disliking storekeeping a little more every day. When I was free to sell it, I did, and went to raising cattle. And one day, riding in a canyon after strayed steers, I found—I think—Aunt Bessie. A cowboy who worked for me was along, or I would never have let anybody know.

We found weathered bones near a little spring. They had a mystery on them, those nameless human bones suddenly come upon. I could feel old death brushing my back.

"Some prospector," suggested my riding partner.

I thought so too until I found, protected by a log, sodden scraps of fabric that might have been a dark, respectable dress. And wrapped in them was a sodden something that might have once been a picture.

The man with me was young, but he had heard the

story of the captive child. He had been telling me about it, in fact. In the passing years it had acquired some details that surprised me. Aunt Bessie had become once more a fair-haired beauty, in this legend that he had heard, but utterly sad and silent. Well, sad and silent she really was.

I tried to push the sodden scrap of fabric back under the log, but he was too quick for me. "That ain't no shirt, that's a dress!" he announced. "This here was no prospector—it was a woman!" He paused and then announced with awe, "I bet you it was your Indian aunt!"

I scowled and said, "Nonsense. It could be anybody."

He got all worked up about it. "If it was my aunt," he declared, "I'd bury her in the family plot."

"No," I said, and shook my head.

We left the bones there in the canyon, where they had been for forty-odd years if they were Aunt Bessie's. And I think they were. But I would not make her a captive again. She's in the family album. She doesn't need to be in the family plot.

If my guess about why she left us is wrong, nobody can prove it. She never intended to join her son in hiding. She went in the opposite direction to lure pursuit away.

What happened to her in the canyon doesn't concern me, or anyone. My Aunt Bessie accomplished what she set out to do. It was not her life that mattered, but his. She bought him another year.

The Hanging Tree

1

Just before the road dipped down to the gold camp on Skull Creek, it crossed the brow of a barren hill and went under the out-thrust bough of a great cottonwood tree.

A short length of rope, newly cut, hung from the bough, swinging in the breeze, when Joe Frail walked that road for the first time, leading his laden horse. The camp was only a few months old, but someone had been strung up already, and no doubt for good cause. Gold miners were normally more interested in gold than in hangings. As Joe Frail glanced up at the rope, his muscles went tense, for he remembered that there was a curse on him.

Almost a year later, the boy who called himself Rune came into Skull Creek, driving a freight wagon. The dangling length of rope was weathered and raveled then. Rune stared at it and reflected, If they don't catch you, they can't hang you.

Two weeks after him, the lost lady passed under the tree, riding in a wagon filled with hay. She did not see the bough or the raveled rope, because there was a bandage over her eyes.

Joe Frail looked like any prospector, ageless, anonymous and dusty, in a fading red shirt and shapeless jeans. His matted hair, hanging below his shoulders, would have been light brown if it had been clean. A long mustache framed his mouth, and he wore a beard because he had not shaved for two months.

The main difference between Joe Frail and any other newcomer to Skull Creek was that inside the pack on his plodding horse was a physician's satchel.

"Now I wonder who got strung up on that tree," remarked his partner. Wonder Russell was Joe Frail's age—thirty—but not of his disposition. Russell was never moody and he required little from the world he lived in. He wondered aloud about a thousand things but did not require answers to his questions.

"I wonder," he said, "how long it will take to dig out a million dollars."

I wonder, Joe Frail thought, if that is the bough from which I'll hang. I wonder who the man is that I'll kill to earn it.

They spent that day examining the gulch, where five hundred men toiled already, hoping the colors that showed in the gravel they panned meant riches. They huddled that night in a brush wickiup, quickly thrown together to keep off the rain.

"I'm going to name my claim after me when I get one," said Wonder Russell. "Call it the Wonder Mine."

"Meaning you wonder if there's any pay dirt in it," Joe Frail answered. "I'll call mine after myself, too. The Frail Hope."

"Hell, that's unlucky," his partner objected.

"I'm usually unlucky," said Joe Frail.

He lay awake late that first night in the gulch, still shaken by the sight of the dangling rope. He remembered the new-made widow, six years ago, who had shrieked a prophecy that he would sometime hang.

Before that, he had been Doctor Joseph Alberts, young and unlucky, sometimes a prospector and sometimes a physician. He struck pay dirt, sold out and went back East to claim a girl called Sue, but she had tired of waiting and had married someone else. She sobbed when she told him, but her weeping was not because she had spoiled her life and his. She cried because she could not possess him now that he was rich.

So he lost some of his youth and all his love and even his faith in love. Before long he lost his riches, too, in a fever of gambling that burned him up because neither winning nor losing mattered.

Clean and new again, and newly named Frail—he chose that in a bitter moment—he dedicated himself to medicine for a winter. He was earnest and devoted, and when spring came he had a stake that would let him go prospecting again. He went north to Utah to meet a man named Harrigan, who would be his partner.

On the way, he camped alone, he was held up and robbed of his money, his horse and his gun. The robbers, laughing, left him a lame pinto mare that a Digger Indian would have scorned.

Hidden in a slit in his belt for just such an emergency was a twenty-dollar gold piece. They didn't get that.

In Utah he met Harrigan—who was unlucky, too. Harrigan had sold his horse but still had his saddle and forty dollars.

"Will you trust me with your forty dollars?" Joe Frail asked. "I'll find a game and build it bigger."

"I wouldn't trust my own mother with that money," Harrigan objected as he dug into his pocket. "But my mother don't know how to play cards. What makes you think you do?"

"I was taught by an expert," Joe Frail said briefly.

In addition to two professions, doctor and miner, he had two great skills: he was an expert card player and a top hand with a pistol. But he played cards only when he did not care whether he won or lost. This time winning was necessary, and he knew what was going to happen—he would win, and then he would be shattered.

He found a game and watched the players—two cowboys, nothing to worry about; a town man, married, having a mildly devilish time; and an older man, probably an emigrant going back East with a good stake. The emigrant was stern and tense and had more chips before him than anyone else at the table.

When Doc sat in, he let the gray-haired man keep winning for a while. When the emigrant started to lose, he could not pull out. He was caught in some entangling web of emotions that Doc Frail had never felt.

Doc lost a little, won a little, lost a little, began to win. Only he knew how the sweat ran down inside his dusty shirt.

The emigrant was a heavy loser when he pulled out of the game.

"Go to find my wife," was his lame excuse. But he went only as far as the bar and was still there, staring into the mirror, when Doc cashed in his chips and went out with two hundred dollars in his pockets.

He got out to the side of the saloon before the shakes began.

"And what the hell ails you?" Harrigan inquired. "You won."

"What ails me," said Doc with his teeth chattering, "is that my father taught me to gamble and my mother taught me it was wicked. The rest of it is none of your business."

"You sound real unfriendly," Harrigan complained. "I was admiring your skill. It must be mighty handy. The way you play cards, I can't see why you waste your time doctoring."

"Neither can I," said Doc.

He steadied himself against the building. "We'll go someplace and divide the money. You might as well have yours in your pocket."

Harrigan warned, "The old fellow, the one you won from, is on the prod."

Doc said shortly, "The man's a fool."

Harrigan sounded irritated. "You think everybody's a fool."

"I'm convinced of it."

"If you weren't one, you'd clear out of here," the cowboy advised. "Standing here, you're courting trouble."

Doc took that as a challenge. "Trouble comes courting me, and I'm no shy lover."

He felt as sore as raw meat. Another shudder shook him. He detested Harrigan, the old man, himself, everybody.

The door swung open and the lamplight showed the gray-haired emigrant. The still night made his words clear: "He cheated me, had them cards marked, I tell you!"

Salt stung unbearably on raw meat. Doc Frail stepped forward.

"Are you talking about me?"

The man squinted. "Certainly I'm talking about you. Cheating, thieving tinhorn—"

Young Doc Frail gasped and shot him.

Harrigan groaned, "My God, come on!" and ducked back into darkness.

But Doc ran forward, not back, and knelt beside the fallen man as the men inside the saloon came cautiously out.

Then there was a woman's keening cry, coming closer. "Ben! Ben! Let me by—he's shot my husband!"

He never saw her, he only heard her wailing voice. "You don't none of you care if a man's been killed, do you! You'll let him go scot free and nobody cares. But he'll hang for this, the one who did it! You'll burn in hell for this, the lot of you—"

Doc Frail and Harrigan left that place together—the pinto carried both saddles and the men walked. They parted company as soon as they could get decent horses, and Doc never saw Harrigan again.

A year or so later, heading for a gold camp, Doc met the man he called Wonder, and Wonder Russell, it seemed to him, was the only true friend he had ever had.

But seeing him for the first time, Joe Frail challenged him with a look that warned most men away, a slow, contemptuous look from hat to boots that seemed to ask, "Do you amount to anything?"

That was not really what it asked, though. The silent question Joe Frail had for every man he met was "Are you the man? The man for whom I'll hang?"

Wonder Russell's answer at their first meeting was as silent as the question. He smiled a greeting, and it was as if he said, "You're a man I could side with."

They were partners from then on, drifting through good luck and bad, and so finally they came to Skull Creek.

They built more than one wickiup in the weeks they spent prospecting there, moving out from the richest part of the strike, because that was already claimed.

By September they were close to broke.

"A man can go to work for wages," Wonder Russell suggested. "Same kind of labor as we're doing now, only we'd get paid for it. I wonder what it's like to eat."

"You'll never be a millionaire working someone else's mine," Doc warned.

I wonder how a man could get a stake without working, his partner mused.

"I know how," Joe Frail admitted. "How much have we got between us?"

It added up to less than fifty dollars. By morning of the following day, Joe Frail had increased it to almost four hundred and was shuddering so that his teeth chattered.

"What talent!" Wonder Russell said in awe. He asked no questions.

Four days after they started over again with a new supply of provisions, they struck pay dirt. They staked two claims, and one was as good as the other.

"Hang on or sell out?" Joe Frail asked.

"I wonder what it's like to be dirty rich," Wonder mused. "On the other hand, I wonder what it's like to be married?"

Joe Frail stared. "Is this something you have in mind for the immediate future, or are you just dreaming in a general kind of way?"

Wonder Russell smiled contentedly. "Her name is Julie and she works at the Big Nugget."

And she already has a man who won't take kindly to losing her, Joe Frail recollected. Wonder Russell knew that as well as he did.

She was a slim young dancer, beautiful though haggard, this Julie at the Big Nugget. She had tawny hair in a great knot at the back of her neck, and a new red scar on one shoulder; it looked like a knife wound and showed when she wore a low-necked dress.

"Let's sell, and I'll dance at your wedding," Joe Frail promised.

They sold the Wonder and the Frail Hope on a Monday and split fifteen thousand dollars between them. They could have got more by waiting, but Wonder said, "Julie don't want to wait. We're going out on the next stage, Wednesday."

"There are horses for sale. Ride out, Wonder." Doc could not forget the pale, cadaverous man called Dusty Smith who would not take kindly to losing Julie. "Get good horses and start before daylight."

"Anybody'd think it was you going to get married, you're in such a sweat about it," Wonder answered, grinning. "I guess I'll go tell her now."

A man should plan ahead more, Joe Frail told himself. I planned only to seek for gold, not what to do if I found it, and not what to do if my partner decided to team up with someone else.

He was suddenly tired of being one of the anonymous, bearded, sweating toilers along the creek. He was tired of being dirty. A physician could be clean and wear good clothes. He could have a roof over his head. Gold could buy anything—and he had it.

He had in mind a certain new cabin. He banged on the door until the owner shouted angrily and came with a gun in his hand.

"I'd like to buy this building," Joe Frail told him. "Right now."

A quarter of an hour later, he owned it by virtue of a note that could be cashed at the bank in the morning, and the recent owner was muttering to himself out in the street, with his possessions on the ground around him, wondering where to spend the rest of the night.

Joe Frail set his lantern on the bench that constituted all the cabin's furniture. He walked over to the wall and kicked it gently.

"A whim," he said aloud. "A very solid whim to keep the rain off."

Suddenly he felt younger than he had in many years, light-hearted, completely carefree, and all the wonderful world was his for the taking. He spent several minutes leaping into the air and trying to crack his heels together three times before he came down again. Then he threw back his head and laughed.

Lantern in hand, he set out to look for Wonder. When he met anyone, as he walked toward the Big Nugget, he lifted the lantern, peered into the man's face, and asked hopefully, "Are you an honest man?"

Evans, the banker, who happened to be out late, answered huffily, "Why, certainly!"

Wonder Russell was not in the saloon, but tawny-haired Julie was at the bar between two miners. She left them and came toward him smiling.

"I hear you sold out," she said. "Buy me a drink for luck?"

"I'll buy you champagne if they've got it," Joe Frail promised.

When their drinks were before them, she said, "Here's more luck of the same kind, Joe." Still smiling gaily, she whispered, "Go meet him at the livery stable." Then she laughed and slapped at him as if he had said something especially clever, and he observed that across the room Dusty Smith was playing cards and carefully not looking their way.

"I've got some more places to visit before morning," Joe Frail announced. "Got to find my partner and tell him we just bought a house."

He blew out the lantern just outside the door. It was better to stumble in the darkness than to have Dusty, if he was at all suspicious, be able to follow him conveniently.

Wonder was waiting at the livery stable corral.

"Got two horses in here, paid for and saddled," Wonder reported. "My war sack's on one of 'em, and Julie's stuff is on the other."

"I'll side you. What do you want done?"

"Take the horses out front of the Big Nugget. They're yours and mine, see? If anybody notices, we bought 'em because we made our pile and we've been drinking. Hell, nobody'll notice anyway."

"You're kind of fidgety," Joe Frail commented. "Then what?"

"Get the horses there and duck out of sight. That's

all. I go in, buy Julie a drink, want her to come out front and look at the moon."

"There isn't any moon," Joe warned him.

"Is a drunk man going to be bothered by that?" Wonder answered. "I'll set 'em up for the boys and then go show Julie the moon while they're milling around. That's all."

"Good luck," Joe Frail said, and their hands gripped. "Good luck all the way for you and Julie."

"Thanks, partner," Wonder Russell said.

And where are you going, friend? Joe Frail wondered. Your future is none of my business, any more than your past.

He staggered as he led the horses down the gulch, in case anyone was watching. A fine performance, he told himself; too bad it is so completely wasted. Because who's going to care, except Dusty Smith, if Julie runs off and gets married?

He looped the lines over the hitch rail so that a single pull would dislodge them. Then he stepped aside and stood in the shadows, watching the door.

Wonder Russell came out, singing happily: "Oh, don't you remember sweet Betsy from Pike, who crossed the big desert with her lover Ike?"

Another good performance wasted, Joe Frail thought. The lucky miner with his claim sold, his pockets full of money, his belly full of whiskey—that was Wonder's role, and nobody would have guessed that he was cold sober.

Wonder capped his performance by falling on the

steps and advising them to get out of the way and let a good man pass. Joe grinned and wished he could applaud.

Two men came out and, recognizing Russell, loudly implored him to let some golden luck rub off on them. He replied solemnly, "Dollar a rub, boys. Every little bit helps." They went away laughing as he stumbled through the lighted doorway.

Joe Frail loosened his guns in their holsters and was ready in the shadows. The best man helps the happy couple get away, he remembered, but this time not in a shower of rice with tin cans tied to the buggy and bunting on the team!

Wonder Russell was in the doorway with Julie beside him, laughing.

"Moon ain't that way," Russell objected. "It's over this way." He stepped toward the side of the platform where the saddled horses were.

Inside the lighted room a white-shirted gaunt man whirled with a gun in his hand, and Dusty Smith was a sure target in the light for three or four seconds while Joe Frail stood frozen with his guns untouched. Then the noise inside the saloon was blasted away by a gunshot, and Wonder Russell staggered and fell.

The target was still clear while Dusty Smith whirled and ran for the back door. A pistol was in Joe Frail's right hand, but the pistol and the hand might as well have been blocks of wood. He could not pull the trigger—until the miners roared their shock and anger and Dusty Smith had got away clean.

Joe Frail stood frozen, hearing Julie scream, seeing the men surge out the front door, knowing that some of them followed Dusty Smith out the back.

There were some shots out there, and then he was no longer frozen. His finger could pull the trigger for a useless shot into the dust. He ran to the platform where Julie was kneeling. He shouldered the men aside, shouting, "Let me by. I'm a doctor."

But Wonder Russell was dead.

"By God, Joe, I wish you'd have come a second sooner," moaned one of the men. "You could have got him from the street if you'd been a second sooner. It was Dusty Smith."

Someone came around the corner of the building and panted the news that Dusty had got clean away on a horse he must have had ready out back.

Joe Frail sat on his heels for a long time while Julie held Wonder's head in her arms and cried. One of the little group of miners still waiting asked, "You want some help, Joe? Where you want to take him?"

He looked down at Julie's bowed head.

My friend—but her lover, he remembered. She has a better right.

"Julie," he said. He stooped and helped her stand up.

"It doesn't matter," she said dully. "To my place, I guess."

Joe Frail commissioned the building of a coffin and bought burying clothes at the store—new suit and shirt that Wonder had not been rich long enough to buy for himself. Then, carrying a pick and shovel, he climbed the hill.

While he was digging, another friend of Wonder's came, then two more, carrying tools of the same kind.

"I'd rather you didn't," Joe Frail told them. "This is something I want to do myself."

The men nodded and turned away.

When he stopped to rest, standing in the half-dug grave, he saw another man coming up. This one, on horseback, said without dismounting, "They got Dusty hiding about ten miles out. Left him for the wolves."

Joe Frail nodded. "Who shot him?"

"Stranger to me. Said his name was Frenchy Plante."

Joe went back to his digging. A stranger had done what he should have done, a stranger who could have no reason except that he liked killing.

Joe Frail put down his shovel and looked at his right hand. There was nothing wrong with it now. But when it should have pulled the trigger, there had been no power in it.

Because I shot a man in Utah, he thought, I can't shoot any more when it matters.

Julie climbed the hill before the grave was quite finished. She looked at the raw earth, shivering a little in the wind, and said, "He's ready."

Joe stood looking at her, but she kept her eyes down.

"Julie, you'll want to go away. You'll have money to go on—all the money for his claim. I'll ride with you as far as Elk Crossing, so you'll have someone to talk to if you want to talk. I'll go with you farther than that if you want."

"Maybe. Thanks. But I kind of think I'll stay in Skull Creek."

She turned away and walked down the hill.

Sometime that night, Julie cut her throat and died quietly and alone.

2

Elizabeth Armistead, the lost lady, came to Skull Creek the following summer.

About four o'clock one afternoon, a masked man rode out of the brush and held up a stage coach some forty miles south of the diggings. Just before this, the six persons aboard the stage were silently wrapped in their separate thoughts, except the stage line's itinerant blacksmith, who was uneasily asleep.

A tramp printer named Heffernan was dreaming of riches to be got by digging gold out of the ground. A whiskey salesman beside him was thinking vaguely of suicide, as he often did during a miserable journey. The driver, alone on his high seat, squinted through glaring light and swiped his sleeve across his face, where sand scratched the creases of his skin. He envied the passengers, protected from the sand-sharp wind and was glad he was quitting the company. He was going back to Pennsylvania, get himself a little farm. Billy McGinnis was fifty-eight years old on that last day of his life.

The sick passenger, named Armistead, was five years older and was planning to begin a career of schoolteaching in Skull Creek. He had not intended to go there. He had thought he had a good thing in Elk Crossing, a more stable community with more children who needed a school. But another wandering scholar had got there ahead of him, and so he and his daughter Elizabeth traveled on toward the end of the world.

The world ended even before Skull Creek for Mr. Armistead.

His daughter Elizabeth, aged nineteen, sat beside him with her hands clasped and her eyes closed but her back straight. She was frightened, had been afraid for months, ever since people began to say that Papa was dishonest. This could not be, must not be, because Papa was all she had to look after and to look after her.

Papa was disgraced and she was going with him into exile. She took some comfort from her own stubborn, indignant loyalty. Papa had no choice, except of places to go. But Elizabeth had had a choice—she could have married Mr. Ellerby and lived as she had always lived, in comfort.

If Papa had told her to do so, or even suggested it, she would have married Mr. Ellerby. But he said it was for her to decide and she chose to go away with

Papa. Now that she had an idea how harsh life could be for both of them, she was sick with guilt and felt that she had been selfish and willful. Mr. Ellerby had been willing to provide Papa with a small income, as long as he stayed away, and she had deprived him of it.

These two had no real idea about what the gold camp at Skull Creek would be like. The towns they had stopped in had been crude and rough, but they were at least towns, not camps. Some of the people in them intended to stay there, and so made an effort toward improvement.

Mr. Armistead was reasonably certain that there were enough children in Skull Creek for a small private school and he took it for granted that their parents would be willing to pay for their education. He assumed, too, that he could teach them. He had never taught or done any other kind of work, but he had a gentleman's education.

He was bone-tired as well as sick and hot and dusty, but when he turned to Elizabeth and she opened her eyes, he smiled brightly. She smiled back, pretending that this endless, unendurable journey to an indescribable destination was a gay adventure.

He was a gentle, patient, hopeful man with good intentions and bad judgment. Until his financial affairs went wrong, he had known no buffeting. Catastrophe struck him before he acquired the protective calluses of the spirit that accustomed misfortune can produce.

All the capital they had left was in currency in a small silk bag that Elizabeth had sewed under her long, full traveling dress.

Elizabeth was wondering, just before the holdup, whether her father could stand it to travel the rest of the days and all night on the final lap of the journey. But the stage station would be dirty and the food would be horrible—travel experience had taught her to be pessimistic—and probably it would be better if they went on at once to Skull Creek where everything, surely, would be much, much pleasanter. Papa would see to that. She could not afford to doubt it.

Billy McGinnis, the driver, was already in imagination in Pennsylvania when a masked rider rode out of scanty timber at his right and shouted, "Stop there!"

Billy had been a hero more than once in his career, but he had no leanings that way any more. He cursed dutifully but hauled on the lines and stopped his four horses.

"Drop that shotgun," the holdup man told Billy. He obeyed, dropping the weapon carefully, making no startling movement.

"Everybody out!" yelled the masked man. "With your hands up."

The printer, as he half fell out of the coach (trying to keep his hands up but having to hang on with one of them), noted details about the bandit: tall from the waist up but sort of short-legged, dusty brown hat, dusty blue shirt, red bandanna over his face.

The whiskey salesman stumbled out hastily—he had

been through this a couple of times before and knew better than to argue—and wondered why a man would hold up a stage going into a gold camp. The sensible thing was to hold up one going out.

The blacksmith, suddenly wide awake, was the third to descend. He accepted the situation philosophically, having no money with him anyway, and not even a watch.

But Mr. Armistead tried to defend his daughter and all of them. He warned her, "Don't get out of the coach."

As he stepped down, he tried to fire a small pistol he had brought along for emergencies like this.

The bandit shot him.

Billy McGinnis, jerking on the lines to hold the frightened horses, startled the masked man into firing a second shot. As Billy pitched off the seat, the team lit out running, with Elizabeth Armistead screaming in the coach.

She was not in it any more when the three surviving men found it, overturned, with the frantic horses tangled in the lines, almost an hour later.

"Where the hell did the lady go to?" the blacksmith demanded. The other two agreed that they would have found her before then if she had jumped or fallen out during the runaway.

They did the best they could. They shouted and searched for another hour, but they found no sign of the lost lady. At the place where the coach had turned over, there was no more brush or scrubby timber by the road, only the empty space of the Dry Flats, dotted with greasewood.

One of the horses had a broken leg, so the whiskey salesman shot it. They unhitched the other three, mounted and searched diligently, squinting out across the flats, calling for the lost lady. But they saw nothing and heard no answering cry.

"The sensible thing," the printer recommended, "is to get on to the station and bring out more help."

"Take the canteen along?" suggested the whiskey salesman.

"If she gets back here, she'll need water," the blacksmith reminded him. "And she'll be scared. One of us better stay here and keep yelling."

They drew straws for that duty, each of them seeing himself as a hero if he won, the lady's rescuer and comforter. The blacksmith drew the short straw and stayed near the coach all night, with the canteen, but the lady did not come back.

He waited alone in the darkness, shouting until he grew hoarse and then voiceless. Back at the place of the holdup, Billy McGinnis and Mr. Armistead lay dead beside the road.

Doc Frail was shaving in his cabin, and the boy called Rune was sullenly preparing breakfast, when the news came about the lost lady.

Doc Frail was something of a dandy. In Skull Creek, cleanliness had no connection with godliness and neither did anything else. Water was mainly used for washing gold out of gravel, but Doc shaved every morning or had the barber do it.

Since he had Rune to slave for him, Doc had his boots blacked every morning and started out each day with most of the dried mud brushed off his coat and breeches. He was a little vain of his light brown curly hair, which he wore hanging below his shoulders. Nobody criticized this, because he had the reputation of having killed four men.

The reputation was unearned. He had killed only one, the man in Utah. He had failed to kill another, and so his best friend had died. These facts were nobody's business.

Doc Frail was quietly arrogant, and he was the loneliest man in the gold camp. He belonged to the aristocracy of Skull Creek, to the indispensable men like lawyers, the banker, the man who ran the assay office, and saloon owners. But these men walked in conscious rectitude and carried pistols decently concealed. Doc Frail wore two guns in visible holsters.

The other arrogant ones, who came and went, were the men of ill will, who dry-gulched miners on their way out with gold. They could afford to shoulder lesser men aside. Doc Frail shouldered nobody except with a look.

Where he walked, other men moved aside, greeting him respectfully: "Morning, Doc. . . . How are you, Doc? Hear about the trouble down the gulch, Doc?"

He brandished no pistol (though he did considerable target practice, and it was impressively public) and said nothing very objectionable. But he challenged with a look.

His slow gaze on a stranger, from hat to boots, asked silently, "Do you amount to anything? Can you prove it?"

That was how they read it, and why they moved aside.

What he meant was, "Are you the man I'm waiting for, the man for whom I'll hang?" But nobody knew that except himself.

By Skull Creek standards, he lived like a king. His cabin was the most comfortable one in camp. It had a wood floor and a half partition to divide his living quarters from his consulting room.

The boy Rune, bent over the cookstove, said suddenly, "Somebody's hollering down the street."

"That's a fact," Doc answered, squinting in his shaving mirror.

Rune wanted, of course, to be told to investigate, but Doc wouldn't give him the satisfaction and Rune wouldn't give Doc the satisfaction of doing anything without command. The boy's slavery was Doc's good joke, and he hated it.

There was a pounding on the door and a man's voice shouting, "Doc Frail!"

Without looking away from his mirror, Doc said, "Well, open it," and Rune moved to obey.

A dusty man shouldered him out of the way and announced, "Stage was held up yestiddy, two men killed and a lady lost track of."

Doc wiped his razor and permitted his eyebrows to go up. "She's not here. One of us would have noticed."

The messenger growled. "The boys thought we better warn you. If they find her, you'll be needed."

"I'll keep it in mind," Doc said mildly.

"They're getting up a couple posses. I don't suppose you'd care to go?"

"Not unless there's a guarantee I'd find the lady. What's the other posse for?"

"To get the road agent. One of the passengers thinks he'd recognize him by the build. The driver, Billy McGinnis, was shot, and an old man, the father of the lost lady. Well, I'll be going."

The messenger turned away, but Doc could not quite let him go with questions still unasked.

"And how," he inquired, "would anybody be so careless as to lose a lady?"

"Team ran off with her in the coach," the man answered triumphantly. "When they caught up with it, she wasn't in it any more. She's lost somewheres on the Dry Flats."

The boy Rune spoke unwillingly, unable to remain silent and sullen: "Kin I go?"

"Sure," Doc said with seeming fondness. "Just saddle your horse."

The boy closed down into angry silence again. He had no horse; he had a healing wound in his shoulder and a debt to Doc for dressing it. Before he could have anything he wanted, he had to pay off in service his debt to Doc Frail—and the service would end only when Doc said so.

Doc Frail set out after breakfast to make his rounds—a couple of gunshot wounds, one man badly burned from falling into his own fire while drunk, a baby with colic, a miner groaning with rheumatism, and a dance-hall girl with a broken leg resulting from a fall off a table.

The posses were setting out then with considerable confusion and some angry arguments over the last of the horses available at the livery stable.

"You can't have that bay!" the livery stable man was shouting. "That's a private mount and I dassent rent it!"

"You certainly dassent," Doc agreed. "The bay is mine," he explained to three scowling men. The explanation silenced them.

Doc had an amusing thought. Rune would sell his soul to go out with the searchers.

"Get the mare ready," Doc said, and turned back to his cabin.

"I've decided to rent you my horse," he told the sullen boy. "For your services for—let's see—one month in addition to whatever time I decide you have to work for me anyway."

It was a cruel offer, adding a month to a time that might be endless. But Rune, sixteen years old, was a gambler. He blinked and answered, "All right."

"Watch yourself," Doc warned, feeling guilty. "I don't want you crippled." The wound was two weeks old.

"I'll take good care of your property," the boy promised. "And the horse too," he added, to make his meaning clear.

Doc Frail stood back, smiling a little, to see which crowd Rune would ride with. There was no organized law enforcement in the gravel gulches of Skull Creek, only occasional violent surges of emotion, with mob anger that usually dissolved before long.

If I were that kid, thought Doc, which posse would I choose, the road agent or the lady? He watched the boy ride to the milling group that was headed for the Dry Flats and was a little surprised. Doc himself would have chosen the road agent, he thought.

So would Rune, except that he planned to become a road agent himself if he ever got free of his bondage.

Rune dreamed, as he rode in the dust of other men's horses, of a bright, triumphant future. He dreamed of a time when he would swagger on any street in any town and other men would step aside. There would be whispers: "Look out for that fellow. That's Rune."

Doc Frail's passage in a group earned that kind of honor. Rune, hating him, longed to be like him.

Spitting dust, the boy dreamed of more immediate glory. He saw himself finding the lost lady out there on the Dry Flats in some place where less keen-eyed searchers had already looked. He saw himself comforting her, assuring her that she was safe now.

He was not alone in his dreaming. There were plenty of dreams in that bearded, ragged company of gold-seekers (ragged even if they were already rich, bedraggled with the dried mud of the creek along which sprawled the diggings). They were men who lived for tomorrow and the comforts they could find somewhere else when, at last, they pulled out of Skull Creek. They were rough and frantic seekers after fortune, stupendously hard workers, out now on an unaccustomed holiday.

Each man thought he was moved by compassion, by pity for the lost and lovely and mysterious lady whose name most of them did not yet know. If they went instead because of curiosity and because they needed change from the unending search and labor in the gravel gulches, no matter. Whatever logic moved them, they rode out to search, fifty motley, bearded men, each of whom might find the living prize.

Only half a dozen riders had gone over the sagebrush hills to look for the road agent who had killed two men. The miners of Skull Creek gambled for fortune but, except when drunk, seldom for their lives. About the worst that could happen in looking for the lost lady was that a man might get pretty thirsty. But go looking for an armed bandit—well, a fellow could get shot. Only the hardy adventurers went in that posse.

When the sun went down, nobody had found anybody, and four men were still missing when the rest of the lady's seekers gathered at the stage line's Station Three. The state company superintendent permitted a fire to be set to a pile of stovewood (freighted in at great expense, like the horse feed and water and everything else there) to make a beacon light. The missing men came in swearing just before midnight. Except for a few provident ones, most of the searchers shivered in their broken sleep, under inadequate and stinking saddle blankets.

They were in the saddle, angry and worried, before dawn of the day Elizabeth Armistead was found.

The sun was past noon when black-bearded Frenchy Plante stopped to tighten his cinch and stamp his booted feet. He pulled off a blue kerchief that protected his nose and mouth from the windborne grit, shook the kerchief and tied it on again. He squinted into the glare and, behind a clump of greasewood, glimpsed movement.

A rattler, maybe. Might as well smash it. Frenchy liked killing snakes. He had killed two men, too, before coming to Skull Creek, and one since—a man whose name he found out later was Dusty Smith.

He plodded toward the greasewood, leading his horse, and the movement was there—not a rattler but the wind-whipped edge of a blue skirt.

"Hey!" he shouted, and ran toward her.

She lay face down, with her long, curling hair, once glossy brown, dull and tangled in the sand. She lay flat and drained and lifeless, like a dead animal. Elizabeth Armistead was not moving. Only her skirt fluttered in the hot wind.

"Lady!" he said urgently. "Missus, here's water."

She did not hear. He yanked the canteen from his

saddle and pulled out the stopper, knelt beside her and said again, "Lady, I got water."

When he touched her shoulder, she moved convulsively. Her shoulders jerked and her feet tried to run. She made a choking sound of fear.

But when he held the canteen to her swollen, broken lips, she had life enough to clutch at it, to knock it accidentally aside so that some of the water spilled on the thankless earth. Frenchy grabbed the canteen and set it again to her lips, staring at her face with distaste.

Dried blood smeared it, because sand cut into the membranes of the nose like an abrasive. Her face was bloated with the burn of two days of sun, and her anguished lips were shapeless.

Frenchy thought, I'd rather be dead. Aloud he said, "No more water now for a minute. Pretty soon you can have more, Missus."

The lost lady reached blindly for the canteen, for she was blind from the glaring sun, and had been even before she lost her bonnet.

"You gotta wait a minute," Frenchy warned. "Don't be scared, Missus. I'm going to fire this here gun for a signal, call the other boys in. We'll get you to the stage station in no time."

He fired twice into the air, then paused. Two shots meant "found dead." Then he fired the third that changed the pattern and told the other searchers, listening with their mouths open slightly, that the lady had been found living.

The first man to get there was tall, fair-haired Rune,

aching with sunburn and the pain of his wound, which had pulled open. When Frenchy found the lady, Rune had been just beyond a little rise of barren ground, stubbornly dreaming as he rode.

I should have been the one, he thought with dull anger. I should have been the one, but it's always somebody else.

He looked at the lady, drained and half dead, dull with dust. He saw the frail and anxious hands groping for the canteen, clutching it as Frenchy guided it to her mouth. He saw the burned, blind face. He said, "Oh, God!"

Frenchy managed a friendly chuckle.

"You're going to be all right, Missus. Get you to a doctor right away. That's a promise, Missus. Frenchy Plante's promise."

He put his name on her, he staked his claim, Rune thought. Who cares? She's going to die anyway.

"I'll go for Doc," Rune said, turning his horse toward the stage station.

But he couldn't go for Doc, after all. He took the news to Station Three; he had that much triumph. Then there was vast confusion. The stage line superintendent ordered a bed made up for the lady, and it was done—that is, the stocktender took the blankets off his bunk and gave them a good shaking and put them back on again. Riders began to come in, shouting, "How is she? Who found her?"

By the time Frenchy Plante arrived, with the lady limp in his arms, and an escort of four other searchers who had gone in the direction of his signal shots, it was discovered that nobody at all had started for Skull Creek to get the doctor.

Rune sat on the ground in the scant shade of the station with his head bowed on his knees, as near exhausted as he had ever been in his life. His shoulder wound hurt like fury, and so did his stomach whenever he remembered how the lost lady looked.

Frenchy Plante was the hero again. He borrowed a fresher horse and rode on to Skull Creek.

He found Doc Frail at home but occupied with a patient, a consumptive dancer from the Big Nugget. With her was another woman, who looked up scowling, as Doc did, when Frenchy came striding in.

"Found the lady, Doc," Frenchy announced. "Want you to come right away."

"I have a patient here," Doc said in controlled tones, "as you will see if you're observant. This lady also needs me."

The consumptive girl, who had seldom been called a lady, was utterly still, lying on Doc's own cot. Her friend was holding her hands, patting them gently.

"Come out a minute," Frenchy urged, "so I can tell you." Doc closed the door behind him and faced Frenchy in the street.

Frenchy motioned toward the door. "What's Luella doing in your place?"

"Dying," Doc answered. "She didn't want to do it where she works."

"How soon can you come? The lost lady's real bad.

Got her to the stage station, but she's mighty sick."

"If she's as sick as this one," Doc said, "it wouldn't do her any good for me to start out there anyway."

"Damned if you ain't a hard-hearted scoundrel," commented Frenchy, half shocked and half admiring. "You ain't doing Luella no good, are you?"

"No. Nobody ever has. But I'm not going to leave her now."

Frenchy shrugged. "How long'll it be?"

"Couple hours, maybe. Do you expect me to strangle her to hurry it along?"

Frenchy's eyes narrowed. "I don't expect nothing. Get out there when you feel like it. I done my duty anyhow."

Was that a reminder, Doc wondered as he watched Frenchy ride on to the Big Nugget, that once you did a duty that should have been mine? That you killed Dusty Smith—a man you didn't even know—after I failed?

Doc Frail went back into his cabin.

A few hours later, Luella released him by dying.

It was dawn when he flung himself off a rented horse at the station and stumbled over a couple of the men sleeping there on the ground.

The lost lady, her face glistening with grease that the stocktender had provided, was quiet on a bunk, with a flickering lamp above her on a shelf. Cramped and miserable on his knees by the bunk was Rune, whose wrist she clutched with one hand. Her other arm cradled Frenchy's canteen.

There was a spot of blood on Rune's shoulder, soaked through Doc's neat dressing, and he was almost too numb to move, but he looked up with hostile triumph.

"She let me be here," he said.

"Now you can go back to Skull Creek," Doc told him, stating a command, not permission. "I'll stay here until she can be moved."

Dispossessed, as he had often been before, but triumphant as he had longed to be, Rune moved away, to tell the sleepy, stirring men that Doc had come. He was amused, when he started back to the gold camp a little later, by the fact that he still rode Doc's mare and Doc would be furious when he discovered it.

The searchers who delayed at Station Three because of curiosity were relieved at the way Doc Frail took charge there. The lost lady seemed to be glad of his presence, too. He treated her burns and assured her in a purring, professional tone, "You'll get your sight back, madam. The blindness is only temporary, I can promise you that."

To the clustering men, he roared like a lion: "Clean this place up—she's got to stay here a few days. Get something decent for her to eat, not this stageline diet. That's enough to kill an ox. Clean it up, I say—with water. Don't raise a lot of dust."

The superintendent, feeling that he had done more than his duty by letting the stocktender feed the search posse, demurred about wasting water.

"Every drop has to be hauled clear from Skull

Creek," he reminded Doc, who snapped back, "Then hitch up and start hauling!"

The stocktender was caught between Doc's anger and the superintendent's power to fire him. He said in a wheedling voice, "Gonna make her some good soup, Doc. I shot a jackrabbit and had him in the pot before he quit kicking."

"Get out of here," snarled Doc. He bent again to the burned, anguished lady.

"You will be able to see again," he promised her. "And your burns will heal."

But your father is dead and buried, and Skull Creek is no place for you, my dear.

3

Frenchy Plante was still around when Rune got back to Skull Creek. Frenchy swaggered, as he had a right to do, being the man who had found the lost lady. But he spent only half a day or so telling the details over. Then he went back to the diggings, far up the gulch, to toil again in the muck and gravel. He had colors there, he was making wages with a small sluice, he had high hopes of getting rich. It had happened before.

The curious of Skull Creek left their own labors to stand by and get the story. When Frenchy was out of the way, Rune became the belligerent center of attention. He had just finished applying a bunchy bandage to his painful shoulder when he jumped guiltily at a pounding on Doc's door. He finished putting his shirt on before he went to take the bar down.

"Doc ain't back yet?" the bearded caller asked. Rune shook his head.

"Expecting him?" the man insisted.

"He don't tell me his plans."

The man looked anxious. "Look here, I got a boil on my neck needs lancing. Don't suppose you could do it?"

"Anybody could do it. Wrong, maybe. Doc could do it right—I guess."

The man sidled in. "Hell, you do it. Ain't he got some doctor knives around, maybe?"

Rune felt flattered to have someone show confidence in him.

"I'll find something," he offered. He did not know the name of the thing he found, but it was thin and sharp and surgical. He wiped it thoroughly on a piece of clean bandage and, after looking over the boil on the man's neck, opened it up with a quick cut.

The patient said, "Wow!" under his breath and shuddered. "Feels like you done a good job," he commented. "Now tie it up with something, eh?"

He stretched out his booted legs while he sat back in Doc's best chair and waited for Rune to find bandaging material that pleased him.

"You was right on the spot when they found her, I hear," he hinted.

"I was second man to get there," Rune answered, pretending that to be second was nothing at all, but knowing that it was something, knowing that the man's boil could have waited, or that anyone could have opened it.

"Heard she's a foreigner, don't talk no English," the man hinted.

"She didn't say nothing to me," Rune answered. "Couldn't talk any language. She's an awful sick lady."

The man touched his bandage and winced. "Well, I guess that fixes it. Your fee the same as Doc Frail's, I suppose?"

As coolly as if he were not a slave, Rune nodded, and the man hauled a poke from his pocket, looking around for the gold scales.

For a little while after he had gone, Rune still hated him, even with the man's payment of gold dust stowed away in his pocket. So easy to get a doctor—or somebody with a knife, anyway—when you had the dust to pay for it! So easy to enter servitude if you were penniless and had to have a shoulder wound dressed and thought you were going to die!

Before the morning was half done, another visitor came. This time it was a woman, and she was alone. The ladies of Skull Creek were few and circumspect, armored with virtue. Rune guessed that this one, wife of Flaunce the storekeeper, would not have visited Doc Frail's office without a companion if she had expected to find Doc there.

But she asked in her prissy way, “Is the doctor in?” and clucked when Rune shook his head.

“Well, I can see him another day,” she decided. “It was about some more of that cough medicine he gave me for my little ones.”

And what for do they need cough medicine in warm weather? Rune would have liked to ask her. He said only, “He ain’t here.”

“He’s out at the stage station, I suppose, with the poor lady who was rescued. Have you heard how she’s getting along?”

“She’s alive but blind and pretty sick,” he said. “She’ll get her sight back afterwhile.”

“I don’t suppose anyone knows why she was coming here?” the woman probed.

“Was with her pa, that’s all I know. He’s dead and she can’t talk yet,” Rune reported, knowing that what Flaunce’s wife really wanted to know was, Is she a lady or one of those others? Was he really her father?

“Dear me,” she asked, “is that blood on your shirt?”

Another one, then, who did not know his shame.

“I shot a rabbit, ma’am,” he lied. That satisfied her, even though a man would not normally carry a freshly killed rabbit over his shoulder.

The woman decided the cough medicine could wait and minced up the deep-rutted street of the gulch, carefully looking neither to right nor left.

At the store, buying supplies for Doc’s account, Rune inquired, “Any news of the other posse? Them that was after the road agent?”

"It's bigger'n it was, now they found the lost lady. Some of the men figure there's got to be a lesson taught."

"If they catch him, that is," Rune suggested, and the storekeeper nodded, sighing, "If they catch him."

In Doc's absence, Rune carried out a project he had in mind, now that there was no fear of interruption by Doc himself. He searched with scrupulous care for the place where Doc hid his gold.

There should be some in the cabin somewhere. Doc had much more than a physician's income, for he had grub-staked many miners, and a few of them had struck it rich. Doc could afford to be careless with his little leather pokes of nuggets and dust, but apparently he wasn't careless. Rune explored under every loose board and in every cranny between the logs, but he didn't find anything. He did not plan to take the gold yet anyway. It could wait until he was free to leave.

And why don't I pull out now? he wondered. Two men that morning had asked if he wanted to work for wages, and he had turned them down.

It was not honor that kept him there—he couldn't afford the luxury of honor. It was not his wound; he knew now he wasn't going to die of that. The reason he was going to stay, he thought, was just because Doc expected him to run out. He would not give his master that much satisfaction.

He was Rune, self-named, the world's enemy. The world owed him a debt that he had never had much luck in collecting.

He thought he was going to collect when he came to Skull Creek in triumph driving a freight team and carrying his whole fortune—eighty dollars in gold—inside a canvas belt next to his skin. He drew his pay, had a two-dollar meal, and set out for the barber shop.

There was music coming from the Big Nugget. He went in to see the source. Not for any other purpose; Rune spent no money that he didn't have to part with. He did not mean to gamble, but while he watched, a miner looked up and said, scowling, "This is a man's game."

He began to lose, and he could not lose, he must not lose, because if you did not have money you might as well be dead.

When he left the saloon, he was numb and desperate and dead.

Toward morning he tried to rob a sluice. He was not yet hungry, but he would be hungry sometime. He had been hungry before and he was afraid of it. He lurked in shadows, saw the sluice had no armed guard. He was scrabbling against the lower riffles, feeling for nuggets, when a shot came without warning. He fell, pulled himself up and ran, stumbling.

Twenty-four hours later he came out of hiding. He was hungry then, and his shoulder was still bleeding. By that time, he knew where the doctor lived, and he waited, huddling outside the door, while the sun came up.

Doc, in his underwear, opened the door at last to get

his lungs full of fresh air and, seeing the tall boy crouching on the step, said, "Well!" Noticing the blood-stiffened shirt he stepped back, sighing, "Well, come in. I didn't hear you knock."

Rune stood up carefully, trying not to move the injured shoulder, holding it with his right hand.

"I didn't knock," he said, hating this man of whom he must ask charity. "I can't pay you. But I got hurt."

"Can't pay me, eh?" Doc Frail was amused. "Guess you haven't heard that the only patients who didn't pay me are buried up on the hill."

Rune believed his grim joke.

"You've been hiding out with this for quite a spell," Doc guessed, as he teased the shirt away from the wound, and the boy shuddered. "You wouldn't hide out without a reason, would you?"

He was gentle from habit, but Rune did not recognize gentleness. He was being baited and he was helpless. He gave a brazen answer:

"I got shot trying to rob a sluice."

Doc, working rapidly, commented with amusement, "So now I'm harboring a criminal! And doing it for nothing, too. How did you figure on paying me, young fellow?"

The patient was too belligerent, needed to be taken down a peg.

"If I could pay you, I wouldn't have tackled the sluice, would I?" the boy demanded. "I wouldn't have waited so long to see you, would I?"

"You ask too damn many questions," Doc grunted.

"Hold still. . . . Your wound will heal all right. But of course you'll starve first."

Sullen Rune made no answer.

Doc Frail surveyed him. "I can use a servant. A gentleman should have one. To black his boots and cook his meals—you can cook, I hope?—and swamp out the cabin."

Rune could not recognize kindness, could not believe it, could not accept it. But that the doctor should extract service for every cent of a debt not stated—that he could understand.

"For how long?" he bargained, growling.

Doc Frail could recognize what he thought was ingratitude.

"For just as long as I say," he snapped. "It may be a long time. It may be forever. If you bled to death, you'd be dead forever."

That was how they made the bargain. Rune got a home he needed but did not want to accept. Doc got a slave who alternately amused and annoyed him. He resolved not to let the kid go until he learned to act like a human being—or until Doc himself became too exasperated to endure him any more. Rune would not ask for freedom, and Doc did not know when he would offer it.

There was one thing that Rune wanted from him: skill with a gun. Doc's reputation as a marksman trailed from him like a tattered banner. Men walked wide of him and gave him courtesy.

But I won't lower myself by asking him to teach me,

Rune kept promising himself. There were depths to which even a slave did not sink.

A letter came from Doc Frail the day after Rune returned to Skull Creek. It was brought by a horseback rider who came in from Station Three ahead of the stage.

Rune had never before in his life received a letter, but he took it as casually as if he had had a thousand. He turned it over and said, "Well, thanks," and turned away, unwilling to let the messenger know he was excited and puzzled.

"Ain't you going to read it?" the man demanded. "Doc said it was mighty important."

"I suppose you read it already?" Rune suggested.

The man sighed. "I can't read writing. Not that writing, anyhow. Print, now, I can make out with print, but not writing. Never had much schooling."

"He writes a bad hand," Rune agreed, mightily relieved. "Maybe the store man, he could make it out."

So there was no need to admit that he could not read, either. Even Flaunce, the storekeeper, had a little trouble, tracing with his finger, squinting over his glasses.

Doc had no suspicion that his servant could not read. He had never thought about the matter. If he had known, he might not have begun the letter, "White Sambo."

Hearing that, his slave reddened with shame and anger, but the store man merely commented, "Nickname, eh? 'White Sambo: Miss Elizabeth Armistead will arrive in Skull Creek in three or four days. She is still weak and blind. She must have shelter and care. I will provide the care, and the shelter will have to be in the cabin of the admirable and respectable Ma Fisher across the street from my own mansion.

" 'Convey my regards to Mrs. Fisher and make all the necessary arrangements. Nothing will be required of Mrs. Fisher except a temporary home for Miss Armistead, who will of course pay for it.' "

The storekeeper and the messenger stared at Rune. "I'm glad it ain't me that has to ask Ma Fisher a thing like that," the messenger remarked. "I'd as soon ask favors of a grizzly bear."

Flaunce was kinder. "I'll go with you, son. She wants a sack of flour anyhow, over to the restaurant. I'll kind of back you up—or pick up the pieces."

Ma Fisher served meals furiously in a tent restaurant to transients and miners who were tired of their own cooking in front of the wickiups along the gulch. She seldom had any hired help—too stingy and too hard to get along with, it was said. Her one luxury was her cabin, opposite Doc's, weather-tight and endurable even in cold weather. Most of the population, willing to live miserably today in the hope of a golden tomorrow, housed itself in shacks or lean-to's or caves dug into the earth, eked out with poles and rocks and sods.

Ma Fisher fumed a little when she was informed that the lost lady would be her guest, but she was flattered, and besides she was curious.

"I won't have time to wait on her, I want that understood," she warned. "And I won't stand for no foolishness, either."

"She's too sick for foolishness, I'd say," the storekeeper said soothingly. "Hasn't got her sight back yet. She mighty near died out there, you know."

"Well," Ma Fisher agreed without enthusiasm. "Well."

The first words Elizabeth Armistead spoke in the stage station were, faintly, "Where is Papa?"

"Your father is dead," Doc Frail answered gently. "He was shot during the holdup."

Why didn't she know that? She had seen it happen.

She answered with a sigh: "No." It was not an exclamation of shock or grief. It was a soft correction. She refused to believe, that was all.

"They buried him there by the road, along with the driver," Doc Frail said.

She said again, with more determination, "No!" And after a pause she pleaded, "Where is Papa?"

"He is dead," Doc repeated. "I am sorry to tell you this, Miss Armistead."

He might as well not have told her. She did not accept it.

She waited patiently in darkness for someone to give a reasonable explanation for her father's absence. She did not speak again for several hours because of her weakness and because of her swollen, broken lips.

Doc wished he could give her the comfort of a sponge bath, but he did not dare offend her by offering to do so himself, and she was not strong enough to move her arms. She lay limp, sometimes sleeping.

When he judged that the girl could better bear the trip to Skull Creek in a wagon than she could stand the stage station any longer, he explained that she would stay at Mrs. Fisher's—a very respectable woman, she would be perfectly safe there—until she could make plans for going back East.

"Thank you," the lost lady answered. "And Papa is in Skull Creek waiting?"

Doc frowned. The patient was beginning to worry him. "Your father is dead, you know. He was shot in the holdup."

She did not answer that.

"I will try again to comb your hair," Doc offered. "Tomorrow you can wash, if you want to try it. There will be a blanket over the window, and one over the door, and I will be outside to make sure no one tries to come in."

Her trunk was there, brought from the wrecked coach. He searched out clean clothes that she could put on, and carefully he combed her long, dark, curling hair. He braided it, not very neatly, and wound the two thick braids up over her head.

4

The wagon was slow, but Doc Frail preferred it for his patient; she could ride easier than in the coach. He ordered the wagon bed well padded with hay, and she leaned back against hay covered with blankets. He had a canvas shade rigged to protect her from the sun. The stageline superintendent himself was the driver—mightily relieved to be getting this woman to Skull Creek where she would be no more concern of his.

Doc Frail had not looked ahead far enough to expect the escort that accompanied them the last mile of the journey. He sat with the lost lady in the wagon bed, glaring at the curiously silent miners who came walking or riding or who stood waiting by the road.

None of them spoke, and there was no jostling. They only stared, seeing the lady in a blue dress, with a white cloth over her eyes. From time to time, the men nearest the wagon fell back to let the others have their turn.

Once, Doc got a glimpse of the boy Rune, lanky and awkward, walking and staring with the rest. Doc scowled, and the boy looked away.

For a while, the doctor closed his eyes and knew how it must be for the girl who could hear but could not see. The creak of the wagon, the sound of the horses' hoofs—too many horses; she must know they were accompanied. The soft sound of many men's feet walking. Even the restless sound of their breathing.

The lady did not ask questions. She could not hide. Her hands were clasped tightly together in her lap.

"We have an escort," Doc murmured. "An escort of honor. They are glad to see that you are safe and well."

She murmured a response.

At the top of the hill, where the road dipped down to the camp, they lost their escort. The riders and the walkers stepped aside and did not follow. Doc Frail glanced up as the wagon passed under the great, outthrust bough of the gnarled tree and felt a chill tingle the skin along his spine.

Well, the fellow deserved the hanging he would get. Doc regretted, however, that the mob that would be coming in from the north would have to pass Ma Fisher's cabin to reach the hanging tree. He hoped they would pass in decent silence. But he knew they would not.

Rune waited near the tree with the other men, torn between wanting to help the lost lady into the cabin and wanting to see the road agent hang. Whichever thing he did, he would regret not having done the other. He looked up at the great bough, shivered, and decided to stay on the hill.

He could see Doc and the stage superintendent help Miss Armistead down from the wagon. As they took her into Ma Fisher's cabin, he could see something else: dust in the distance.

A man behind him said, "They're bringing him in."

Rune had two good looks at the road agent before he died and one brief, sickening glance afterward. The angry miners were divided among themselves about hanging the fellow. The men who had pursued him, caught him, and whipped him until his back was bloody were satisfied and tired. Four of them even tried to defend him, standing with rifles cocked, shouting, "Back! Get back! He's had enough."

He could not stand; men pulled him off his horse and held him up as his body drooped and his knees sagged.

But part of the crowd roared, "Hang him! Hang him!" and shoved on. The mob was in three parts—those for hanging, those against it, and those who had not made up their minds.

Rune glimpsed him again through the milling miners beneath the tree. The posse men had been pushed away from him, and men who had not pursued him were bringing in a rope.

The black-bearded giant, Frenchy Plante, tied the noose and yanked the road agent to his feet. Frenchy's roar came over the rumbling of the mob: "It's his fault the lost lady pridnear died! Don't forget that, boys!"

That was all they needed. Order came out of chaos. Fifty men seized the rope and at Frenchy's signal "Pull!" jerked the drooping, bloody-backed road agent off the ground. Rune saw him then for the third time, dangling.

A man beside him said knowingly, "That's the most humane way, really—pull him up all standing."

"How do you know?" Rune sneered. "You ever get killed that way?"

With the other men, he walked slowly down the hill. He waited in Doc's cabin until Doc came in.

"You had to watch," Doc said. "You had to see a man die."

"I saw it," Rune growled.

"And the lost lady might as well have. She might as well have been looking, because Ma Fisher kindly told her what the noise was about. And was offended, mind you, when I tried to shut her up!"

Doc unbuckled his gun belt and tossed it on his cot.

"You're going to wait on Miss Armistead," he announced. "I told her you would do her errands, anything that will make her a little easier. Do you hear me, boy? She keeps asking for her father. She keeps saying. 'Where is Papa?' "

Rune stared. "Didn't you tell her he's dead?"

"Certainly I told her! She doesn't believe it. She doesn't remember the holdup or the team running away. All she can remember is that something happened so the coach stopped, and then she was lost, running somewhere, and after a long time a man gave her a drink of water and took the canteen away again."

"Did she say where she's going when she gets her

sight back?" Rune asked.

Doc let out a gusty breath. "She has no place to go. She says she can't go back because she has to wait for Papa. He was going to start a school here, and she was going to keep house for him. She has no place to go, but she can't stay alone in Skull Creek. It's unthinkable."

Ma Fisher came flying over to get Doc.

"The girl's crying and it'll be bad for her eyes," she said.

Doc asked coolly, "And why is she crying?"

"I'm sure I don't know," Ma answered, obviously injured. "I wasn't even talking to her. She started to sob, and when I asked her what was the matter, she said, 'Papa must be dead, or he would have been waiting here to meet me.' "

"Progress," Doc growled. "We're making progress." He went out and left Ma Fisher to follow if she cared to do so.

Doc was up before daylight next morning.

"When Ma Fisher leaves that cabin," Doc told Rune, when he woke him, "you're going to be waiting outside the door. If the lady wants you inside for conversation, you will go in and be as decently sociable as possible. If she wants to be alone, you will stay outside. Is that all perfectly clear?"

It was as clear as it was hateful. Rune would have taken delight in being the lady's protector if he had had any choice. (And Doc would, too, except that he wanted to protect her reputation. It wouldn't look good for him to be in the cabin with her except on brief professional visits.)

"Nursemaid," Rune muttered sourly.

Ma Fisher scowled when she found him waiting outside her door, but Miss Armistead said she would be glad of his company.

The lost lady was timid, helpless, but gently friendly, sitting in the darkened cabin, groping now and then for the canteen that had been Frenchy's.

Rune asked, "You want a cup to drink out of?" and she smiled faintly.

"I guess it's silly," she answered, "but water tastes better from this canteen."

Rune kept silent, not knowing how to answer.

"Doctor Frail told me your first name," the lost lady said, "but not your last."

"Rune is all," he answered. He had made it up, wanting to be a man of mystery.

"But everybody has two names," she chided gently. "You must have another."

She was indeed ignorant of frontier custom or she would not make an issue of a man's name. Realizing that, he felt infinitely superior and therefore could be courteous.

"I made it up, ma'am," he told her. "There's lots of men here go by names they wasn't born with. It ain't a good idea to ask questions about folks' names." Then, concerned lest he might have offended her, he struggled on to make conversation:

"There's a song about it. 'What was your name in

the States? Was it Johnson or Olson or Bates?' Goes that way, sort of."

The lady said, "Oh, my goodness. Doctor Frail didn't make up his name, I'm sure of that. Because a man wouldn't take a name like that, would he?"

"A man like Doc might," Rune decided. The idea interested him. "Doc is a sarcastic fellow."

"Never to me," Miss Armistead contradicted softly. "He is the soul of kindness! Why, he even realized that I might wish for someone to talk to. And you are kind, too, Rune, because you came."

To get her off that subject, Rune asked, "Was there any errands you'd want done or anything?"

"Doctor Frail said he would send my meals in, but I am already so much obligated to him that I'd rather not. Could you cook for me, Rune, until I can see to do it myself?"

"Sure," he agreed. "But I cook for Doc anyhow. Just as easy to bring it across the street."

"No, I'd rather pay for my own provisions." She was firm about that, with the pathetic stubbornness of a woman who for the first time must make decisions and stick to them even if they are wrong.

"I have money," she insisted. "I can't tell what denomination the bills are, of course. But you can tell me."

Poor, silly lady, to trust a stranger so! But Rune honestly identified the bills she held out.

"Take the five dollars," she requested, "and buy me whatever you think would be nice to eat. That much money should last for several days, shouldn't it?"

Rune swallowed a protest and murmured, "Kind of depends on what you want. I'll see what they got at Flaunce's." He backed toward the door.

"I must be very businesslike," Miss Armistead said with determination. "I have no place to go, you know, so I must earn a living. I shall start a school here in Skull Creek."

Arguing about that was for Doc, not for his slave. Rune did not try.

"Doc's going in his cabin now," he reported, and fled across the street for instructions.

The storekeeper's inquisitive wife got in just ahead of him, and he found Doc explaining, "The lady is still too weak for the strain of entertaining callers, Mrs. Flaunce. The boy here is acting as amateur nurse, because she needs someone with her—she can't see, you know. But it would not be wise for anyone to visit her yet."

"I see," Mrs. Flaunce said with cold dignity. "Yes, I understand perfectly." She went out with her head high, not glancing at the cabin across the street.

Doc thus cut the lost lady off from all decent female companionship. The obvious conclusion to be drawn—which Mrs. Flaunce passed on to the other respectable women of the camp—was that the doctor was keeping the mysterious Miss Armistead. Ma Fisher's stern respectability was not enough to protect her, because Ma herself was strange. She chose to earn her living in a community where no sensible woman would stay if she wasn't married to a man who required it.

When Mrs. Flaunce was gone, Rune held out the greenback.

"She wants me to buy provisions with that. Enough for several days, she says."

Doc's eyebrows went up. "She does, eh? With five dollars? Why, that'd buy her three cans of fruit, wouldn't it? And how much is Flaunce getting for sugar, say?"

"Dollar a pound."

Doc scowled thoughtfully. "This is a delicate situation. We don't know how well fixed she is, but she doesn't know anything about the cost of grub in Skull Creek. And I don't want her to find out. Understand?"

Rune nodded. For once, he was in agreement with his master.

Doc reached into his coat pocket and brought out a leather poke of dust.

"Put that on deposit to her account at the store," he ordered.

"Lady coming in on the stage wouldn't have gold in a poke, would she?" Rune warned.

Doc said with approval, "Sometimes you sound real smart. Take it to the bank, get currency for it, and take the currency to Flaunce's. And just pray that Ma Fisher doesn't take a notion to talk about the price of grub. Let the lady keep her stake to use getting out of here as soon as she's able."

A week passed before he realized that Elizabeth Armistead could not leave Skull Creek.

5

Elizabeth could find her way around the cabin, groping, stepping carefully so as not to fall over anything. She circled sometimes for exercise and to pass the long, dark time and because she did not feel strong enough to think about important matters.

The center of her safe, circumscribed world was the sagging double bed where she rested and the table beside it, on which was the water bucket. She still clung to Frenchy Plante's canteen and kept it beside her pillow but only when she was alone so that no one would guess her foolish fear about thirst. But every few minutes she fumbled for the dipper in the bucket. She was dependent on strangers for everything, of course, but most important of them was Rune, who filled the water bucket at the creek that he said was not far outside the back door.

She had explored the cabin until she knew it well, but its smallness and scanty furnishings still shocked her. Papa's house back East had had nine rooms, and until his money began to melt away, there had been a maid as well as a cook.

She moved cautiously from the table a few steps to the front door—rough planks with a strong wooden bar to lock it from the inside; around the wall to a bench that Rune had placed so she would not hurt herself on the tiny stove; then to the back door.

But the need for decision gnawed at her mind and made her head ache.

"You must go back East just as soon as you can travel," Doctor Frail had said—how many times?

But how could she travel again when she remembered the Dry Flats that had to be crossed? How could she go without Papa, who was dead, they kept telling her?

The cabin was uncomfortably warm, but she could not sit outside the back door, where there was grass, unless Rune was there. And she must not open the door unless she knew for sure who was outside.

She could not go back East yet, no matter what they said. To stay in Skull Creek was, of course, an imposition on these kind people, but everything would work out all right after a while—except for Papa, who they said was dead.

She remembered what Papa had said when his investments were dwindling.

"We do what we must," he had told her with his gentle smile when he made the hard decision to go West. And so his daughter would do what she must.

I must find a place for the school, she reminded herself. Perhaps Mrs. Fisher will let me use this cabin. I must offer her pay, of course, very tactfully so she will not be offended.

It was a relief to keep her mind busy in the frightening darkness, safe in the cabin with an unknown, raucous settlement of noisy men just outside the door. There were women, too; she could hear their laughter and screaming sometimes from the saloon down the street. But ladies did not think about those women except to pity them.

They were very strange, these people who were looking after her—Doc, who sounded strained and cross; Rune, whose voice was sullen and doubtful; Mrs. Fisher, who talked very little and came to the cabin only to groan into bed. Elizabeth was a little afraid of all of them, but she reminded herself that they were really very kind.

There was cautious knocking on the door, and she called out, "Yes?" and turned. Suddenly she was lost in the room, not sure of the position of the door. Surely the knocking was at the back? And why should any of them come that way, where the little grassy plot went only down to the creek?

She stumbled against a bench, groping. The knocking sounded again as she reached the door. But she was cautious. "Who is it?" she called, with her hand on the bar.

A man's voice said, "Lady! Lady, just let me in."

Elizabeth stopped breathing. The voice was not Doc Frail's nor Rune's. But it was cordial, enticing: "Lady, you ever seen a poke of nuggets? I got a poke of gold right here. Lady, let me in."

She trembled and sank down on the floor in her darkness, cowering. The voice coaxed, "Lady? Lady?"

She did not dare to answer. She did not dare to cry. After a long time the pounding and the coaxing stopped.

She could not escape any more by planning for the school. She was remembering the long horror of thirst, and the noise the mob had made, going past to hang a man on a tree at the top of the hill. She hid her burned face in her trembling hands, crouching by the barred door, until a familiar and welcome voice called from another direction, "It's me. Rune."

She groped to the front door, reached for the bar. But was the voice familiar and therefore welcome? Or was this another importunate, lying stranger? With her hand on the unseen wooden bar, she froze, listening, until he called again. His voice sounded concerned: "Miss Armistead, are you all right in there?"

This was Rune. She could open the door. He was not offering a poke of nuggets, he was only worried about her welfare.

"I was frightened," she said as she opened the door.

"You're safer that way in Skull Creek," he said. "Anything you want done right now?"

"You are so kind," she said gently. "No, there is nothing. I have plenty of drinking water in the bucket. Oh—if you go to the store, perhaps there would be some potatoes and eggs?"

After a pause he said, "I'll ask 'em." (A month ago there had been a shipment of eggs; Doc had mentioned it. There had not been a potato in camp since Rune came there.)

"Doc says to tell you you'll have your unveiling this evening, get your eyes open. I got to go find him now, give him a message from the Crocodile."

"The—what?"

"Ma Fisher, I mean." She could hear amusement in his voice.

"Why, it's not nice to speak of her so. She is very kind to me, letting me share her home!"

There was another pause. He said, "Glad to hear it," and "I'll go find Doc now. He went to get a haircut."

Doc's haircut was important. He went often to the barbershop for a bath, because he could afford to be clean, but never before in Skull Creek had he let scissors touch his hair, hanging in glossy waves below his shoulders.

A miner might let his hair and whiskers grow, bushy and matted, but Doc Frail was different. His long hair was no accident, and it was clean. He wore it long as a challenge, a quiet swagger, as if to tell the camp, "You may make remarks about this if you want trouble." Nobody did in his presence.

Except the barber, who laughed and said, "I been wantin' to put scissors to that, Doc. You gettin' all fixed up for the lost lady to take a good look?"

Doc had dignity even in a barber's chair. "Shut up and tend to business," he advised. There was no more conversation even when the barber handed him a mirror.

Rune had too much sense to mention the reformation. The tall boy glanced at him, smiled tightly, and reported, "Ma Fisher wants to see you. She's tired of having the lost lady underfoot."

Doc snorted. "Ma has no weariness or distaste that a poke of dust won't soothe." He turned away, but Rune was not through talking.

"Can I come when you take the bandage off her eyes?"

"No. Yes. What do I care?" Doc strode away, trying to put his spirits into a suitably humble mood to talk business with Ma Fisher.

The girl was a disturbing influence for him, for Rune, for the whole buzzing camp. She must get out in a few days, but she must not be made any more miserable than she already was.

He did not wait for Ma Fisher to attack, from her side of the dirty wooden counter in her tent restaurant. He spoke first: "You would no doubt like to be paid for Miss Armistead's lodging. I will pay you. I don't want you to get the idea that I'm keeping her. My reason for wishing to pay is that I want her to keep thinking the world is kind and that you have welcomed her."

Ma Fisher shrugged. "You can afford it. It's an inconvenience to me to have her underfoot."

Doc put a poke on the counter. "You can heft that if you want to. That's dust you'll get for not letting her know she's unwelcome. You'll get it when she leaves, in a week or so."

Ma lifted the leather sack with an expert touch. "All right."

Doc swept it back again. "One compliment before I leave you, Mrs. Fisher: you're no hypocrite."

"Two-faced, you mean? One face like this is all a woman can stand." She cackled at her own wit. "Just the same, I'd like to know why you're willing to pay good clean dust to keep the girl from finding out the world is cruel."

"I wish I knew myself," he answered.

I'll take off the dressings now, he decided, and let her get a glimpse of daylight, let her see what she's eating for a change.

He crossed the street and knocked, calling, "Doc Frail here." Rune opened the door.

Elizabeth turned her face toward him. "Doctor? Now will you let me see again? I thought if you could take the dressings off now, you and Rune might be my guests for supper."

You and Rune. The leading citizen and the unsuccessful thief.

"I'll be honored," Doc replied. "And I suppose Rune realizes that it is an honor for him."

He removed the last dressings from her eyes and daubed the closed lids with liquid.

"Blink," he ordered. "Again. Now try opening them."

She saw him as a blurred face, close up, without distinguishing characteristics. The one who protected in the darkness, the one who had promised to bring light. The only dependable creature in the world. There was light again, she had regained her sight. She must trust him, and she could. He had not failed her in anything.

But he was a stranger in a world of terror and strangers. He was too young. A doctor should be old, with a gray chin beard.

"Hurts a little?" he said. "You can look around now."

He stepped aside and she was lost without him. She saw someone else, tall in the dimness; that was Rune, and he was important in her life. She tried to smile at him but could not tell whether he smiled back.

Doc said, "Don't look in a mirror yet. When your face is all healed, you will be a pretty girl again. Don't worry about it."

Unsmiling, she answered, "I have other things to concern me."

Elizabeth tried to make conversation as they ate the supper Rune had cooked. But now that she could see them dimly, they were strangers and she was lost and afraid.

"It's like being let out of jail, to see again," she offered. "At least I suppose it is. When may I go outside to see what the town is like?"

"There is no town, only a rough camp," Doc told her. "It's not worth looking at, but you may see it tomorrow. After sunset, when the light won't hurt your eyes."

The following day, after supper, when she heard knocking on the front door, she ran to answer. Dr. Frail had changed his mind about waiting until later, she assumed. He must have come back sooner than he had expected from a professional call several miles away.

She swung the door wide—and looked up through a blur into the black-bearded, grinning face of a stranger. Then she could not shut it again. A lady could not do a thing so rude as that.

The man swept off his ragged hat and bowed awkwardly. "Frenchy Plante, ma'am. You ain't never seen me, but we sure enough met before. Out on the Dry Flats."

"Oh," she said faintly. He looked unkempt and she could smell whiskey. But he had saved her life. "Please come in," she said, because there was no choice. She hoped he did not notice that she left the door open. With this man in the cabin, she wanted no privacy.

He remembered to keep his hat in his hand but he sat down without waiting to be invited.

"Figure on doing a little prospecting, ma'am," he said jovially. "So I just dropped in to say good-by and see how you're making out."

Frenchy was well pleased with himself. He was wearing a clean red shirt, washed though not pressed, and he had combed his hair, wanting to make a good impression on the lost lady.

"I have so much to thank you for," Elizabeth said earnestly. "I am so very grateful."

He waved one hand. "It's nothing, lady. Somebody would of found you." Realizing that this detracted from his glory, he added, "But of course it might have been too late. You sure look different from the first time I seen you!"

Her hands went up to her face. "Doctor Frail says there won't be any scars. I wish I could offer you some refreshment, Mr. Plante. If you would care to wait until I build up the fire to make tea?"

Doc Frail remarked from the doorway, "Frenchy would miss his afternoon tea, I'm sure."

There were a few men in the camp who were not afraid of Doc Frail—the upright men, the leading citizens, and Frenchy Plante.

Frenchy had the effrontery to suggest, "Come on in, Doc," but the wisdom to add, "Guess I can't stay, ma'am. Going prospecting, like I told you."

Doc Frail stood aside so as not to bar his progress in leaving. "I thought your claim was paying fairly well."

Frenchy made an expansive gesture. "Sold it this morning. I want something richer."

Elizabeth said, "I hope you'll find a million dollars, Mr. Plante."

"With a pretty lady like you on my side, I can't fail, can I?" replied the giant, departing.

Elizabeth put on her bonnet. With her foot on the threshold, she murmured, "Everyone is so kind." She took Doc's arm as he offered it.

"To the left," he said. "The tougher part of the camp is to the right. You must never go that way. But this is the way you will go to the hotel, where the stage stops.

Next week you will be able to leave Skull Creek."

She did not seem to hear him. She trembled. She was staring with aching eyes at the rutted road that led past Flaunce's store and the livery stable, the road that took a sudden sweep upward toward a cottonwood tree with one great out-thrust bough.

"You are perfectly safe," Doc reminded her. "We will not go far this time. Only past the store."

"No!" she moaned. "Oh, no!" and tried to turn back.

"Now what?" Doc demanded. "There is nothing here to hurt you."

But up there where she had to go sometime was the hanging tree, and beyond was the desert. Back all that distance, back all alone—a safe, quiet place was what she must have now, at once.

Not here in the glaring sun with the men staring and the world so wide that no matter which way she turned she was lost, she was thirsty, burning, dying.

But there must be some way out, somewhere safe, the cool darkness of a cabin, if she could only run in the right direction and not give up too soon—

But someone tried to keep her there in the unendurable sun glare with the thirst and endless dizzying space—someone held her arms and said her name urgently from far away as she struggled.

She jerked away with all her strength because she knew the needs of her own anguished body and desperate spirit—she had to be free, she had to be able to hide.

And where was Papa, while this strange and angry

man carried her back to the cabin that was a refuge from which she would not venture forth again?

And who was this angry boy who shouted, "Doc, if you've hurt her, I'll kill you!"

When she was through with her frantic crying and was quiet and ashamed, she was afraid of Doc Frail, who gripped her wrists as she lay on Ma Fisher's bed.

"What was it, Elizabeth?" he demanded. "Nothing is going to hurt you. What did you think you saw out there?"

"The Dry Flats," she whispered, knowing he would not believe it. "The glaring sun on the Dry Flats. And I was lost again and thirsty."

"It's thirty miles to the Dry Flats," he told her brusquely. "And the sun went down an hour ago. It's getting dark here in the gulch."

She shuddered.

"I'll give you something to make you sleep," he offered.

"I want Papa," she replied, beginning to cry again.

Back in his own cabin, Doc walked back and forth, back and forth across the rough floor boards, with Rune glaring at him from a corner.

Doc Frail was trying to remember a word and a mystery. Someone in France had reported something like this years ago. What was the word, and what could you do for the suffering patient?

He had three books in his private medical library, but they treated of physical ailments, not wounds of the mind. He could write to Philadelphia for advice, but—he calculated the weeks required for a letter to go East and a reply to come back to Skull Creek.

"Even if they know," he said angrily, "we'll be snowed in here before the answer comes. And maybe nobody knows, except in France, and he's probably dead now, whoever he was."

Rune spoke cuttingly. "You had to be in such a hurry to make her start back home!"

Doc said, "Shut your mouth."

What was the word for the mystery? Elizabeth remembered nothing about the runaway of the coach horses, nothing about the holdup that preceded it, only the horror that followed.

"Hysteria?" he said. "Is that the word? Hysteria? But if it is, what can you do for the patient?"

The lost lady would have to try again. She would have to cross the imaginary desert as well as the real one.

6

I will not try to go out for a few days, Elizabeth told herself, comforted by the thought that nobody would expect her to try again after what had happened on her first attempt.

The desert was not outside the cabin, of course. It was only a dreadful illusion. She realized that, because she could look out and see that the street was in a ravine. Nothing like the Dry Flats.

Next time, she assured herself, it will be all right. I will not look up toward the tree where they—no, I will simply not think about the tree at all, nor about the Dry Flats. Other people go out by stage and nothing happens to them. But I can't go right away.

Doctor Frail did not understand at all. He came over the next morning, implacable and stern.

"I have a patient to see down at the diggings," he said, "but he can wait half an hour. First you will walk with me as far as Flaunce's store."

"Oh, I couldn't," she answered with gentle firmness. "In a few days, but not now. I'm not strong enough."

He put his hat on the table and sat on one of the two benches.

"You will go now, Elizabeth. You have got to do it now. I am going to sit here until you are ready to start."

She stared at him in hurt surprise. Of course he was a doctor, and he could be expected to be always right. He was a determined man, and strength came from him. It was good, really, not to make a decision but to have him make it, even though carrying it out would be painful. Like the time Papa made her go to a dentist to have a tooth pulled.

"Very well," she replied with dignity. She put her bonnet on, not caring that there was no mirror.

"You are only going for a walk to the store," he told her, offering his arm at the door. "You will want to tell your friends back home what a store in a gold camp is like. You will have a great many things to tell your friends."

She managed a laugh as she walked with her eyes down, feeling the men staring.

"They would not believe the things I could tell them," she agreed.

The sun was not yet high over the gulch and the morning was not warm but she was burning and thirsty and could not see anything for the glare and could not breathe because she had been running, but he would not let her fall. He was speaking rapidly and urgently, telling her she must go on. He was not Papa because Papa was never angry; Papa would never have let her be afraid and alone in the glare and thirsty and going to die here, now, if he would only let her give up and fall . . .

She was lying down—where? On the bed in the cabin? And turning her head away from something, the sharp odor of something the doctor held under her nose to revive her.

The men had seen her fall, then, the staring men of Skull Creek, and she had fainted, and they must think she was insane and maybe she was.

She was screaming and Doc Frail was slapping her cheek, saying, "Elizabeth! Stop that!"

Then she was crying with relief, because surely now nobody would make her go out again until she was ready.

The doctor was angry, a cruel man, a hateful stranger. Angry at a helpless girl who needed only to be let alone until she was stronger!

She said with tearful dignity, “Please go away.”

He was sarcastic, too. He answered, “I do have other patients,” and she heard the door close.

But she could not lie there and cry as she wanted to do, because she had to bar the door to keep out fear.

At noontime she was calmer and built a fire in the little stove and brewed some tea to eat with a cold biscuit of the kind Rune called bannock. Nobody came, and in the afternoon she slept for a while, exhausted, but restless because there was a great deal of racket from down the gulch.

Rune leaned against a building with his thumbs in his belt, watching two drunk miners trying to harness a mule that didn’t want to be harnessed. Rune was amused, glad to have something to think about besides Doc Frail’s cruelty to the lost lady.

“Leave her strictly alone till I tell you otherwise,” Doc had commanded.

Rune was willing, for the time being. She had cold grub in the cabin and the water bucket was full. He didn’t want to embarrass her by going there anyway. He had seen her stumble and struggle and fall. He had watched, from Doc’s shack, as Doc carried her back to the cabin, had waited to be called and had been ignored.

The plunging mule kicked one of the miners over backward into the dust, while a scattering of grinning men gathered and cheered.

The other drunk man had a long stick, and as he

struck out with it, the mule went bucking, tangled in the harness. A man standing beside Rune commented with awe and delight, "Right toward Ma Fisher's restaurant! Now I'd admire to see that mule tangle with her!"

He shouted, and Rune roared with him. A roar went up from all the onlookers as the far side of Ma Fisher's tent went down and Ma came running out on the near side, screaming. The mule emerged a few seconds behind her, but the drunk miner was still under the collapsed, smoke-stained canvas.

There was a frenzied yell of "Fire!" even before Rune saw the smoke curl up and ran to the nearest saloon to grab a bucket.

They kept the flames from spreading to any buildings although the lean-to behind the tent was badly charred and most of the canvas burned.

Ma Fisher was not in sight by the time they got the fire out. Rune slouched away, grinning.

Ma Fisher made only one stop on the way from her ruined restaurant to the cabin. She beat with her fist on the locked door of the bank until Mr. Evans opened it a few inches and peered cautiously out.

"I want to withdraw all I've got on deposit," she demanded. "I'm going to my daughter's in Idaho."

He unfastened the chain on the inside and swung the door open.

"Leaving us, Mrs. Fisher?"

"Sink of iniquity," she growled. "Of course I'm leaving. They've burned my tent and ruined my stove, and now they can starve for all I care. I want to take out every dollar.

"But you needn't think I want to carry it with me on the stage," she warned. "I just want to make the arrangements now. Transfer it or whatever you do, so's I can draw on it in Idaho."

"Will you need some for travel expenses?" the banker asked, opening his ledger.

"I've got enough dust on hand for that. Just let me sign the papers and get started."

Rune, lounging in Doc's doorway, saw Ma Fisher jerk at her own door handle and then beat angrily with her fists, yelling, "Girl, you let me in! It's Ma Fisher."

She slammed the door behind her, and Rune grinned. He worried a little though, wondering how her anger would affect the gentle Miss Armistead. But he had his orders not to go over there. His own opinion was that the lost lady was being mighty stubborn, and maybe Doc Frail was right in prescribing the let-alone treatment till she got sensible.

Elizabeth listened with horror to Ma Fisher's description of the wrecking of her restaurant. Ma paced back and forth across the floor and she spat out the news.

"How dreadful!" Elizabeth sympathized. "What can I do to help you?"

Ma Fisher stopped pacing and stared at her. It was a long time since anyone had offered sympathy. Having had little of it from anyone else, she had none to give.

“I don’t need nothing done for me,” she growled. “I’m one to look after myself. Oh, lawd, the cabin. I’ve got to sell this cabin.”

“But then you’ll have no place to live!” Elizabeth cried out.

“I’m going to Idaho. But I got to get my investment out of the cabin. You’ll have to leave, Miss. I’m going tomorrow on the stage.”

She was pacing again, not looking to see how Elizabeth was affected by the news, not caring, either.

“Man offered me five hundred dollars in clean dust for it not long ago, but I turned it down. Had to have a place to live, didn’t I? Now who was that? Well, it won’t be hard to find a buyer. . . . You’ve got your things all over the place. You better start packing. Could come on the same stage with me if you’re a mind to.”

Out into the open, away from refuge? Out across the Dry Flats—and before that, under the hanging tree? When she could not even go as far as Flaunce’s store!

There was no one to help her, no one who cared what became of her. The doctor was angry, the boy Rune had deserted her, and this hag, this witch, thought only of her own interests. Papa had said, “We do what we must.”

“I will give you five hundred dollars for the cabin,” Elizabeth said coolly.

Doc Frail did not learn of the transaction until noon the next day. He had been called to a gulch ten miles away to care for a man who was beyond help, dying of a self-inflicted gunshot wound. Crippled with rheumatism, the man had pulled the trigger of his rifle with his foot.

Doc rode up to his own door and yelled, "Rune! Take care of my horse."

Rune came around from the back with the wood-chopping axe in his hand.

"Hell's broke loose," he reported. "Old lady Fisher left on the stage this morning, and the girl must be still in the cabin, because she didn't go when Ma did."

Doc sighed.

"Fellow that came by said she's bought Ma's cabin," Rune said, watching to see how Doc Frail would take that news.

Doc disappointed him by answering, "I don't care what she did," and went into his own building.

But while Rune was taking the mare to the livery stable, Doc decided he did care. He cared enough to cross the road in long strides and pound on the door, shouting, "Elizabeth, let me in this instant."

She had been waiting for hours for him to come, to tell her she had done the right thing, the only thing possible.

But he said, "If what I hear is true, you're a fool. What are you going to do in Skull Creek?"

She stepped back before the gale of his anger. She drew herself up very straight.

"Why, I am going to start a school for the children," she replied. "I have been making plans for it all morning."

"You can't. You can't stay here," Doc insisted.

"But I must, until I am stronger."

Doc glared. "You'd better get stronger in a hurry then. You've got to get out of this camp. You can start by walking up to the store. And I'll go with you. Right now."

Elizabeth was angry too. "I thank you for your courtesy," she said. "I must look out for myself now, of course." Looking straight into his eyes, she added, "I will pay your fee now if you will tell me what I owe."

Doc flinched as if she had struck him.

"There is no charge, madam. Call on me at any time." He bowed and strode out.

He told Rune, "The order to leave her alone still stands," and told him nothing else.

Rune endured it for twenty-four hours. The door across the street did not open. There was no smoke from the chimney.

She's got just about nothing in the way of grub over there now, Rune fretted to himself. Ain't even building a fire to make a cup of tea.

But when Rune crossed the street, he did not go for pity. He had convinced himself that his only reason for visiting Elizabeth was that Doc had forbidden him to go there.

He knocked on the slab door but no answer came. He pounded harder, calling, "Miss Armistead!" There was no sound from within, but there was a waiting silence that made his skin crawl.

"It's Rune!" he shouted. "Let me in!"

A miner, passing by, grinned and remarked, "Good luck, boy. Introduce me sometime."

Rune said, "Shut your foul mouth," over his shoulder just as the door opened a crack.

Elizabeth said coolly, "What is it?" Then, with a quick-drawn breath like a sob, "Rune, come in, come in."

As she stepped away from the entrance, her skirt swung and he saw her right hand with a little derringer in it.

"The gun—where'd you get it?" he demanded.

"It was Papa's. They brought it to me with his things after—" Remembering that she must look after herself, not depending on anyone else, she stopped confiding. "Won't you sit down?" she invited formally.

"I just come to—to see how everything is. Like if you needed something."

She shook her head, but her eyes flooded with tears. "Need something? Oh, no. I don't need a thing. Nobody can do anything for me!"

Then she was sobbing, sitting on a bench with her face hidden in her hands, and the little gun forgotten on the floor.

"Listen, you won't starve," he promised. "I'll bring your grub. But have you got money to live on?" He abased himself, admitting, "I ain't got anything. Doc don't pay me. If I had, I'd help you out."

"Oh, no. I will look after myself." She wiped her eyes and became very self-possessed. "Except that for a while I should appreciate it if you will go to the store for me. Until I am strong enough to walk so far myself."

But Doc had said she was strong enough, and Doc Frail was no liar. Rune scowled at Elizabeth. He did not want to be bound to her by pity. It was bad enough to be bound to Doc by debt.

This tie, at least, he could cut loose before it became a serious burden.

"You got to get out of Skull Creek," he said harshly. "Unless you've got a lot of money."

"I have sufficient," she said.

Now she was playing the great lady, he thought. She was being elegant and scornful.

"Maybe where you come from, folks don't talk about such things," he burst out with bitterness. "It ain't nice, you think. Don't think I'm asking how much you got. But you don't know nothing about prices here. You ain't been paying full price for what you got, not by a long ways. You want to know?"

She was staring at him wide-eyed and shocked.

"Sugar's ninety cents a pound at Flaunce's," he told her. "It went down. Dried codfish you're tired of it, I guess, and so's everybody—it's sixty cents. Dried apples—forty cents a pound last time they had any. Maybe you'd like a pound of tea? Two and a half, that costs you. Potatoes and eggs, there ain't been any in a long time. Fresh meat you can't get till another bunch of steers come in. Now how long will your money last you if you stay in Skull Creek?"

She had less than five hundred dollars left after buying the cabin. Stage fare—that was terribly high. She had never had to handle money, and only in the last year had she even had to be concerned about it, since Papa's affairs had gone so badly.

But she said coolly, "I have a substantial amount of money, thank you. And I am going to start a school. Now tell me, please, who paid for my supplies if I didn't?"

Rune gulped. "I can't tell you that."

"So it was Doctor Frail," Elizabeth said wearily. "I will pay him. Tell him that."

"He'd kill me," Rune said. "Remember, I never said it was him."

Between two dangers, the lesser one seemed to be telling Doc himself. He did so at the first opportunity.

Doc did not explode. He only sighed and remarked, "Now she hasn't even got her pride. How much money has she got to live on?"

"She didn't tell me. Won't tell you, either, I'll bet."

"And she thinks she can make a fortune teaching school!" Doc was thoughtful. "Maybe she can earn part of her living that way. How many children are there in camp, anyway?" He scrabbled for a sheet of paper and began writing the names of families, muttering to himself.

"Go to the livery stable," he said without looking up, "and get a string of bells. They've got some. Then figure out a way to hitch them over her door with a rope that she can pull from inside her cabin."

"What for?" Rune demanded.

"So she can signal for help next time somebody tries to break in," Doc explained with unusual patience.

And what will I do to protect her when the time comes? Doc Frail wondered. Look forbidding and let them see two guns holstered and ready? That will not always be enough.

The noted physician of Skull Creek can outshoot anyone within several hundred miles, but will he fire when the target is a man? Never again. Then his hand and his eye lose their cunning, and that is why Wonder Russell sleeps up on the hill. If I could not pull the trigger to save the life of my friend, how can I do it for Elizabeth? I must have a deputy.

Rune was on his way out when Doc asked, "Can you hit a target any better than you dodge bullets?"

Rune hesitated, torn between wanting to boast and wanting to be taught by a master. If he admitted he was no marksman, he was not a complete man. But a slave didn't have to be.

He answered humbly, "I never had much chance to try. Target practice costs money."

"Stop at the store and get a supply of ammunition," Doc ordered. "I'm going to give you the world's best chance to shoot me."

Rune shrugged and went out, admitting no excitement. He was going to have his chance to become the kind of man from whose path other men would quietly step aside.

Doc watched him go, thinking, Are you the one for

whom I'll hang? Put a gun in your hand, and skill with it, and there's no telling. But your lessons start tomorrow.

"I wish the school didn't matter so much to her," Doc muttered. "I wish she wasn't so set on it."

He had made some calls early that morning and was back in his cabin, scowling across the street at Elizabeth's, with its door standing open to welcome the children of Skull Creek.

Her floor was scrubbed; the rough plank table was draped with an embroidered cloth, and her father's books were on it. She visualized the children: shy, adorable, anxious to learn. And their mothers: grateful for a school, full of admonitions about the little ones' welfare, but trusting the teacher.

Doc turned to Rune, saw the rifle across his knees.

"You planning to shoot the children when they come?" he demanded.

"Planning to shoot any miner that goes barging in there with her door open," Rune answered. "Because I don't think there's going to be any children coming to school."

Doc sighed. "I don't either. After all the notes she wrote their mothers, all the plans she made."

At eleven o'clock, they saw Elizabeth shut her door. No one had crossed the threshold.

Doc growled, "Bring my mare. I've got a patient up the gulch. Then go see about getting her dinner."

Rune muttered, "I'd rather be shot."

Elizabeth had the derringer in her hand, hidden in a

fold of her skirt, when she unbarred the door. She did not look at him but simply stepped aside.

"I don't care for anything to eat," she said faintly.

"If you don't eat nothing, I don't either."

She sipped a cup of tea, but she set it down suddenly and began to cry.

"Why didn't anybody come?" she wailed.

"Because they're fools," he told her sturdily.

But he knew why. He had guessed from the way the women acted when he delivered the notes. Elizabeth Armistead, the lost lady, was not respectable. She had come under strange circumstances, and the protection of Doc Frail was like a dark shadow upon her.

"I thought I would teach the children," she said hopelessly. "I thought it would be pleasant."

Rune drew a deep breath and offered her all he had—his ignorance and his pride.

"You can teach me," he said. "I ain't never learned to read."

The look of shock on her face did not hurt quite so much as he had supposed it would.

7

Early cold came to Skull Creek, and early snow. Halfway through one gloomy, endless morning, someone knocked at Elizabeth's door, but she had learned caution. She called, "Who is it?"

A voice she did not know said something about books. When she unbarred the door, the derringer was in her hand, but she kept it decently hidden in the folds of her skirt.

He was a big man with a beard. He swept off a fur cap and was apologetic.

"I didn't mean to frighten you, ma'am. Please don't be afraid. I came to see if you would rent out some of your books."

Elizabeth blinked two or three times, considering the matter. "But one doesn't rent books!" she objected. "I have never heard of renting books . . . It's cold, won't you come in so I can close the door?"

The man hesitated. "If you're sure you will let me come in, ma'am. I swear I'll do you no harm. It's only for books that I came. Some of the boys are about to go crazy for lack of reading matter. We drew straws, and I got the short one. To come and ask you."

It's my house, Elizabeth told herself. And surely no rascal would care for books.

This man happened not to be a rascal, though he acted so fidgety about being in there that Elizabeth wondered who he thought might be chasing him.

"They call me Tall John, ma'am," he said in introduction, cap in hand. "Any book would do, just about. We've worn out the newspapers from the States and we're tired of reading the labels on canned goods. And the winter's only just begun."

He paid five dollars apiece for the privilege of keeping three books for a month. (His listeners, when he read aloud in a hut of poles and earth, were a horse thief, a half-breed Arapaho Indian and the younger son of an English nobleman.)

Doc scolded Elizabeth for letting a stranger in at all, though he admitted that Tall John was a decent fellow.

"He was a perfect gentleman," she insisted. What bothered her was that she had accepted money for lending books.

Rune complained bitterly because his book supply was cut by three.

"Listen, boy," Doc said, "you can read like a house afire, but can you write? Your schooling isn't even well begun. Do you know arithmetic? If you sold me eight head of horses at seventy dollars a head, how much would I owe you?"

"I wouldn't trust nobody to owe me for 'em," Rune told him earnestly. "You'd pay cash on the barrel head, clean dust, or you wouldn't drive off no horses of mine."

But thereafter his daily lessons in Elizabeth's cabin included writing, spelling and arithmetic. When the only books she had left were readers through which he had already ploughed his impetuous way, he was reduced to sneaking a look at the three medical books in Doc's cabin—Doc's entire medical library.

When Rune boasted of how much he was learning in his classes at the lost lady's cabin, Doc listened and was pleased.

"Each week, you will take her a suitable amount of dust for tuition," Doc announced. "I will have to decide how much it's going to be."

"Dust? Where'm I going to get dust?" Rune was frantic; the only delight he had was being barred from him, as everything else was, by his poverty.

"From me, of course. I can properly pay for the education of my servant, surely?"

"The lady teaches me for nothing," Rune said in defense of his privilege. "She don't expect to get paid for it."

"She needs an income, and this will help a little." Doc felt lordly. He was doing a favor for both his charges, Rune and the pathetic girl across the street. "If you don't care to accept a favor from me," he told Rune, "you'd better get used to the idea." With a flash of insight, he explained, "It is necessary sometimes to let other people do something decent for you."

That is, he considered, it is necessary for everybody but me. And I have a sudden very excellent idea about the uses of gold.

He had an interest in several paying placer claims, which he visited often because the eye of the master fatteneth the cattle, and the eye of an experienced gold miner can make a shrewd guess about how many ounces there should be on the sluice riffles at the weekly cleanup. His various partners seldom tried to cheat him any more.

With the ground and the streams frozen, placer mining had come to a dead stop, but Dr. Frail's professional income had dwindled only a little, and there was so much dust to his credit with the bank that he had no financial problems anyway.

He strode up the street to visit Evans, the banker.

"Your dealings with your customers are strictly confidential, are they not?" he inquired.

"As confidential as yours," Evans replied stiffly.

"I want to make a withdrawal. The dust is to be put into leather pokes that can't be identified as the property of anyone around here. Old pokes, well worn."

"Very well," said Evans, as if it happened every day.

"Weigh it out in even pounds," Doc instructed, and Evans' eyebrows went up. "I want—oh, six of them. I'll be back for them this afternoon."

He sat with Elizabeth just before supper, drinking tea, listening to the sounds Rune made chopping firewood outside the back door. Rune had the bags of gold and orders to conceal them in the woodpile to be found accidentally.

"And remember, I know very well how much is in there," Doc had warned him. "I know how much she's supposed to find when she does find it."

Rune had glared at him in cold anger, replying, "Did you think I would steal from *her?*"

Tall John's shack burned when he built the fire too hot on a bitter cold day. The three men who shared it with him were away. He ran out, tried to smother the flames with snow, then ran back to save what he could, and the roof fell in on him.

When help came, he was shouting under the burning

wreckage. His rescuers delivered him to Doc's office with a broken leg and serious burns on his shoulders and chest.

Doc grumbled, "You boys think I'm running a hospital?" and started to work on the patient.

"He's got no place to go; our wickiup burned," the horse thief apologized. "The rest of us, we can hole up some place, but John can't hardly."

"He needs a roof over his head and conscientious nursing," Doc warned.

"I could sort of watch him," Rune suggested, wondering if they would sneer at the idea.

"Guess you'll have to," Doc agreed. "All right, he can have my bunk."

Then there was less company to help Elizabeth pass the time. Rune bought her supplies and carried in firewood, but he was always in a hurry. There were no more interesting evenings with Doc and Rune as her guests for supper, because Doc never stayed with her more than a few minutes.

Winter clamped down with teeth that did not let go. Elizabeth began to understand why Tall John had found it necessary to borrow books—she was reading her father's books over and over to pass the time. She began to understand, too, why a man of pride must pay for such borrowing.

She sewed and mended her own clothes until there was no more sewing to do. Doc commissioned her to make him a shirt and one for Rune. She finished them and was empty-handed again.

Then she peeled every sliver of bark from the logs that made her prison.

Rune came dutifully twice a day to bring supplies, and do her chores, but he no longer had lessons.

"Tall John's teaching me," he explained.

"And what are you studying?" she asked with some coolness.

"Latin. So I can figure out the big words in Doc's books."

"Now I wonder whether Papa brought his Latin grammar," she cried, running to look at the books she could not read.

"You ain't got one," Rune said. "I looked. We get along without. Sometimes we talk it."

"I didn't think anybody talked Latin," Elizabeth said doubtfully.

"Tall John can. He studied it in Rome. Told me where Rome is, too."

Elizabeth sighed. Her pupil had gone far beyond her.

She faced the bleak fact that nobody needed her at all any more. And Doc said there would be at least another month of winter.

"I don't want to impose on you, now that you're so busy," she told Rune with hurt dignity. "Hereafter I will bring in my own firewood and snow to melt for water. It will give me something to do."

"Don't hurt yourself," he cautioned. He didn't seem to see anything remarkable in her resolve to do hard physical labor. Elizabeth had never known any woman who carried water or cut wood. She felt like an adventurer when she undertook it.

Rune told Doc what she was planning, and Doc smiled.

"Good. Then you won't have to find what's in her woodpile. She can find it herself."

He visited her that evening, as he did once a day, briefly. She was a little sulky, he noticed, and he realized that she deserved an apology from him.

"I'm sorry not to spend more time in your company," he said abruptly. "There is no place I'd rather spend it. But for your own protection, to keep you from being talked about—do you understand why I'd rather not be here when Rune can't be here too?"

Elizabeth sniffed. "Have I any good name left to protect?"

The answer was No, but he would not say it.

"Rune says you're going to do your own chores," he remarked.

"Beginning tomorrow," she said proudly, expecting either a scolding or a compliment.

Doc disappointed her by saying heartily, "Good idea. You need some exercise."

Then he wondered why she was so unfriendly during the remainder of his visit.

Her venture into wood cutting lasted three days. Then, with a blister on one hand and a small axe cut in one shoe—harmless but frightening—she began to carry in wood that Rune had already chopped and piled earlier in the winter.

She was puzzled when she found a leather bag, very heavy for its size, and tightly tied. Unable to open the snow-wet drawstring with her mittened hands, she carried the bag into the house and teased the strings open with the point of a knife.

She glimpsed what was inside, ran to the shelf for a plate, and did not breathe again until the lovely yellow treasure was heaped upon it.

"Oh!" she said. "Oh, the pretty!" She ran her chilled fingers through the nuggets and the flakes that were like fish scales. "Maybe it belongs to Ma Fisher," she said angrily to the emptiness of the cabin. "But I bought the place and it's mine now. And maybe there's more out there!"

She found them all, the six heavy little bags, and completely demolished the neat woodpile.

Then she ran to the rope of the warning bells and pulled it for the first time, pulled it again and again, laughing and crying, and was still pulling it when Rune came shouting.

She hugged him, although he had a cocked pistol in his hand. She did not even notice that.

"Look!" she screamed. "Look what I found in the woodpile!"

Doc came to admire, later in the day, and stayed for supper, but Elizabeth was too excited to eat—or to cook, for that matter. The table was crowded, because all the golden treasure was on display in plates or cups. She kept touching it lovingly, gasping with delight.

"Now you know," Doc guessed, "why men search for that. And why they kill for it."

"I know," she crooned. "Yes, I understand."

He leaned across the table. "Elizabeth, with all that for a stake, you needn't be afraid to go out next spring, go home."

She caressed a pile of yellow gold. "I suppose so," she answered, and he knew she was not convinced.

The woodpile was a symbol after that. She restored the scattered sticks to make a neat heap, but did not burn any of them. She went back to chopping wood each day for the fire.

She was hacking at a stubborn, knotty log one afternoon, her skirts soggy with snow, when a man's voice not far behind her startled her into dropping the axe.

He was on the far side of the frozen creek, an anonymous big man bundled up in a huge and shapeless coat of fur.

"It's me, Frenchy," he shouted jovially. "Looks like you're working too hard for a young lady!"

Elizabeth picked up the axe. When the man who once saved your life speaks to you, you must answer, she decided. Especially when you had nobody to talk to any more.

"I like to be in the fresh air," she called.

He waded through the snow. "Let me do that work for you, little lady."

Elizabeth clung to the axe, and he did not come too close.

"Sure having a cold spell," he commented. "Been a bad winter."

This is my own house, Elizabeth told herself. This man saved my life on the Dry Flats.

"Won't you come in and thaw out by the stove?" she suggested. "Perhaps you'd like a cup of tea."

Frenchy was obviously pleased. "Well, now, a day like this, a man can sure use something hot to drink."

Elizabeth felt guilty, ushering him into her cabin by the back way, as if trying to hide her doings from her guardians across the street. But he had come the back way, and not until later did it occur to her that his choice of routes had been because he wanted to avoid being seen.

He sat across the table from her, affable and sociable, waiting for the tea to steep. When his clothing got warmed, he smelled, but a lady could not tell a guest that he should go home and take a bath.

Frenchy had in mind to tell a fine big lie and perhaps to get himself a stake. The lost lady, he guessed, had brought lots of money with her. For her Rune bought the very best supplies available. She was strange, of course, about staying in her cabin all the time, and he had seen her almost fall down in a kind of struggling fit when she went outside. But she was very pretty, and she was nice to him. Doc Frail was her protector, but Frenchy had a strong suspicion that Doc Frail was frail indeed.

Frenchy went into his lie.

"Just can't hardly wait for a warm spell. I got the prettiest little claim you ever seen—colors galore. I'm going to be the rich Mr. Plante, sure enough. That is," he sighed, "if I can just keep eating till the ground thaws."

He blew politely into his tea to cool it.

"Yes, sir," mused Frenchy, "all I need is a grubstake. And whoever stakes me is going to be mighty lucky. That's how Doc Frail made his pile, you know. Grubstaking prospectors."

He did not ask her for anything. He did not suggest that she stake him. She thought of it all by herself.

"Tell me more, Mr. Plante," she said. "Maybe I will stake you."

He argued a little—couldn't possibly accept a stake from a lady. She argued—he must, because she owed him her life, and she would like to get rich. How much did he need?

Anything, anything—but with prices so high—and he'd have to hire labor, and that came high, too.

She calculated wildly. Six pokes of gold, a pound in each one. She had no basis for computing how much a prospector needed.

"I will give you half of what I have," she offered. "And you will give me half the gold you find. I think we should have some sort of written contract, too."

Frenchy was dazzled. He had nothing to lose. He did not expect to have any gold to divide. His luck had been bad for months, and he intended to leave Skull Creek as soon as the weather permitted travel.

He dictated the contract as Elizabeth wrote in her prettiest penmanship, and both of them signed.

"The contract's yours to keep," he told her. It was a valid grubstake contract—if the holder could enforce it.

"I'll name the mine after you," he promised, vastly cheerful. "A few weeks from now—next summer anyway—you'll have to get gold scales to keep track of your take. When you see me again, you can call me Solid Gold Frenchy!"

At the Big Nugget, Frenchy took care to stand at the end of the bar nearest the table where Doc Frail was killing time in a card game.

The bartender was polite to Frenchy because business was poor, but his tone was firm as he warned, "Now, Frenchy, you know you ain't got no more credit here."

Frenchy was jovial and loud in his answer: "Did I say a word about credit this time? Just one drink, and I'll pay for it." He pulled out a poke.

Doc Frail was paying no attention to Frenchy and not much to the game. He took care to be seen in public most evenings, in the vain hope of weakening the camp's conviction that the lost lady was his property. He succeeded only in confusing the men, who felt he was treating her badly by leaving her in solitude.

Frenchy held up his glass and said with a grin, "Here's to the gold that's there for the finding, and here's to my grubstake partner."

Doc could not help glancing up. Frenchy had worn out three or four stakes already. Doc himself had refused him and did not know of a single man in camp who was willing to give him another start.

He looked up to see Frenchy grinning directly at him.

A challenge? Doc wondered. What's he been up to?

A suspicion of what Frenchy had been up to was like a burning coal in his mind.

Are you the man? he thought. Are you, Frenchy Plante, the man for whom I'll hang?

He stayed on for about an hour, until Frenchy had gone. He found Elizabeth in a cheerful mood, mending one of his shirts.

"The tea's been standing and it's strong," she apologized, getting a cup ready for him.

Drinking it, he waited for her to say that Frenchy had been there, but she only asked about Tall John's health. Finally Doc remarked, "Frenchy Plante has suddenly come into comparative riches. He's got a grubstake from somewhere."

Elizabeth said mildly, "Is that so?"

"He said so when he bought a drink just now," Doc added, and Elizabeth was indignant.

"Is that what he's doing with it—drinking it up? I declare, I don't approve. I grubstaked him, if that's what you're trying to find out. But that was so he wouldn't starve and could go on mining when the weather moderates."

Doc said sadly, "Oh, Elizabeth!"

"It was mine," she maintained. "I simply invested some of it. Because I have plenty—and I want more."

Frenchy went on a prolonged, riotous and dangerous

drinking spree. He was so violent that Madame Dewey, who kept the rooms above the Big Nugget, had him thrown out of there—at some expense, because two men were injured in removing him.

When he was almost broke, he really did go prospecting.

Doc and Rune treated Elizabeth with distant courtesy, mentioning casually the less scandalous highlights of Frenchy Plante's orgy. They did not scold, but their courtesy was painful. She had no friends any more, no alternately laughing and sarcastic friend named Joe Frail, no rude but faithful friend named Rune. They were only her physician and the boy who did her errands. She lived in a log-lined, lamp-lit cave, and sometimes wished she were dead.

There was a window by her front door; Rune had nailed stout wooden bars across it on the inside. For privacy, an old blanket was hung over the bars. She could peek through a small hole in the blanket for a narrow glimpse of the street, but nothing ever happened that was worth looking at. To let in daylight by taking the blanket off the window was to invite stares of men who happened to pass by—and sometimes the curious, yearning, snow-bound miners were too drunk to remember that Doc Frail was her protector, or if they remembered, too drunk to care.

One of them, who tried to get in one evening in mid-April, was cunning when he made his plans. He was sober enough to reconnoiter first.

He knew where Doc Frail was—playing cards at the

Big Nugget, bored but not yet yawning. Rune was in Doc's cabin with a lamp on the table, bent over a book. Tall John was limping down the gulch with a lantern to visit friends. And Frenchy Plante, who had some right to the lady because he had found her, was somewhere out in the hills.

The intruder felt perfectly safe about the warning bells. If the lady pulled the rope, there would be no noise, because he had cut the rope.

Elizabeth was asleep on her bed, fully clothed—she slept a great deal, having nothing else to do—when knuckles rapped at the back door and a voice not quite like Doc's called, "Miss Armistead! Elizabeth!"

She sat up, frozen with fright. Then the pounding was louder, with the slow beats of an axe handle. She did not answer, and with senseless anger the man began to chop at the back door.

She ran and seized the bell rope. It slumped loose in her hands. She heard the dry wood crack and splinter. She did not even try to escape by the front door. She reached for the derringer that had been her father's, pointed it blindly and screamed as she pulled the trigger.

Then she was defenseless, but there was no more chopping, no sound at all, until she heard Rune's approaching shout. She was suddenly calm and guiltily triumphant. Making very sure that Rune was indeed Rune, she unbarred the front door and let him in.

"I fired the little gun!" she boasted.

"You didn't hurt anybody," Rune pointed out. The bullet had lodged in the splintered back door. "We'll just wait right here till Doc comes."

But Doc solved no problems when he came. He sat quietly and listened to Elizabeth's story.

"I don't know," Doc said hopelessly. "I don't know how to protect you." He motioned toward the shattered, splintered door. "Rune, fix that. I'll repair the bell rope."

Rune nailed the back door solid again and was noisy outside at the woodpile for a few minutes. When he came back, he said briefly, "Nobody will try that entrance again tonight. I'm going to bring blankets and sleep on the woodpile."

In Doc Frail's cabin he bundled blankets together. He straightened up and blurted out a question: "How much time do I still owe you?"

"Time? That old nonsense. You don't owe me anything. I just wanted to cut you down to size."

"Maybe somebody will cut you down to size some time," Rune said. "I suppose you were never licked in your life. The great Joe Frail, always on top of the heap. It's time you got off it."

Doc said, "Hey! What's this sudden insurrection?"

"All you do is boss Elizabeth around. Why don't you get down on your knees instead? Didn't it ever dawn on you that if you married her, you could take her out of here to some decent place?" Rune was working himself up to anger. "Sure, she'd say she couldn't go, but you could make her go—tie her up and take her out in a wagon if there's no other way. How do you know the only right way to get her out of Skull Creek is to make her decide it for herself? Do you know everything?"

Doc answered, "No, I don't know everything," with new humility. He was silent for a while. "Don't think the idea is new to me. I've considered it. But I don't think she'd have me."

Rune picked up his blankets. "That's what I mean," he said. "You won't gamble unless you're sure you'll win." He slammed the door behind him.

8

When Doc set out to court Elizabeth Armistead, he put his whole heart into it, since this was what he had been wanting to do for a long time anyway. He was deferential and suitably humble. He was gentle. He was kind. And Elizabeth, who had never had a suitor before (except old Mr. Ellerby, who had talked across her head to her father), understood at once what Doc's intentions were.

He crossed the street more often and stayed longer. He came at mealtime, uninvited, and said he enjoyed her cooking. He even cut and carried in firewood. He brought his socks to be mended. They sat in pleasant domesticity at the table, while Elizabeth sewed and sometimes glanced across at him.

In his own cabin, Rune studied with the patient, Tall John.

And fifteen miles away, Frenchy Plante panned gravel. The ground had thawed, and rain made his labors miserable, but Frenchy had a hunch. Ninety-nine times out of a hundred, his hunches didn't pan out, but he trusted them anyway.

On a slope by a stream there was a ragged old tree. Beside it he had a pit from which he had dug gravel that showed occasional colors. He groaned out of his blankets one gray dawn, in his ragged tent, to find that the tree was no longer visible. Its roots washed by rain, it had fallen head first into his pit.

Frenchy swore.

"A sign, that's what it is," he growled. "A sign there wasn't nothing there to dig for. Damn tree filled up my pit. Going to leave here, never go back to Skull Creek."

But he had left a bucket by the tree, and he went for the bucket. The tree's head was lower than its roots, and the roots were full of mud, slick with rain. Mud that shone, even in the gray light.

He tore at the mud with his hands. He shelled out chunks like peanuts, but peanuts never shone so richly yellow. He forgot breakfast, forgot to build a fire, scrabbled in the oozing mud among the roots.

He held in his hand a chunk the size of a small crab-apple, but no crab-apple was ever so heavy.

He stood in the pouring rain with a little golden apple in his muddy hands. He threw his head back so the rain came into his matted beard, and he howled like a wolf at the dripping sky.

He staked his claim and worked it from dawn to dusk for a week, until he was too exhausted by labor and starvation to wash gravel any more. He might have died there in the midst of his riches, because he was too weak to go back to Skull Creek for grub, but he shot an unwary deer and butchered it and fed. The discovery that even he could lose his strength—and thereby his life and his treasure—frightened him. He caught his horse, packed up, and plodded toward Skull Creek, grinning.

He slogged down the gulch at dusk, eager to break the news to Elizabeth Armistead, but he had another important plan. He shouted in front of a wickiup built into the side of the gulch: "Bill you there? It's Frenchy."

The wickiup had been his until he sold it for two bottles of whiskey. Bill Scanlan looked out and said without enthusiasm, "Broke already? Well, we got beans."

A man known as Lame George, lying on a dirty blanket, grunted a greeting.

"Crowded here," he murmured. "But we can make room."

"Anything happening?" Frenchy asked, wolfing cold fried pork and boiled beans.

"Stages ain't running yet. This camp's played out. What'd you find?"

"Some good, some bad. Mostly bad." That was

honest, not that honesty mattered much, and not that prospectors expected it even among friends. "I was thinking about that time the boys drove the mules through the old lady's tent. I bet there ain't been a funny joke like that for a long time."

Lame George said sadly, "There ain't, for a fact. Nothing much to do, nothing to laugh about. We been digging but couldn't raise a color."

"I got a good idea for a funny joke," Frenchy hinted. "On Doc Frail."

Lame George snorted. "Nobody jokes him."

"I'd make it worth a man's while," Frenchy said with great casualness, and Lame George sat up to demand, "What'll you do it with? You find something?"

"What you got, Frenchy?" Scanlan asked tensely.

"The joke," Frenchy reminded them. "What about the joke on Doc?"

"Hell, yes!" Lame George exploded. "Let us in on something good and we'll take our chances on Doc." He glanced at Scanlan, who nodded agreement.

"All I want," Frenchy explained, spreading his hands to show his innocent intentions, "is to make a social call on the lady, Miss Armistead, without getting my head blowed off. Is Tall John still living at Doc's?"

"He got better and moved to a shack. Rune still lives with Doc. But what," Lame George demanded with justifiable suspicion, "do you want with the lady?"

"Wouldn't hurt her for the world. Won't lay a hand

on her. Just want to talk to her." Frenchy added with a grin, "Just want to show her something I found and brought back in my pocket."

They swarmed at him, grabbed his arms, their eyes eager. "You made a strike, Frenchy? Sure you did—and she grubstaked you!"

Elizabeth sat at the table, mending by lamplight. Doc was across from her, reading aloud to their mutual contentment. He sat in comfort, in his shirt sleeves, his coat and gun belt hanging on a nail by the front door. The fire in the cookstove crackled, and the teakettle purred.

Doc chose his reading carefully. In an hour and a half, he worked through portions of the works of Mr. Tennyson and Mr. Browning and, apparently by accident, looked into the love sonnets of William Shakespeare—exactly what he had been aiming at from the beginning.

"Why," Elizabeth asked, "are you suddenly so restless? Are you tired of reading to me?"

Doc discovered that he was no longer sitting. He was walking the floor, and the time had come to speak.

"My name," he said abruptly, "is not really Frail."

She was not shocked. "Why did you choose that one, then?"

"Because I was cynical. Because I thought it suited me. Elizabeth, I have to talk about myself. I have to tell you some things."

She said, "Yes, Joe."

"I killed a man once."

She looked relieved. "I heard it was four men!"

He frowned. "Does it seem to you that one does not matter? It matters to me."

She said gently, "I'm sorry, Joe. It matters to me, too. But one is better than four."

And even four killings, he realized, she would have forgiven me!

He bent across the table.

"Elizabeth, I enjoy your company. I would like to have it the rest of my life. I want to protect you and work for you and love you and—make you happy, if I can."

"I shouldn't have let you say that," she answered quietly. Her eyes were closed, and there were tears on her cheeks. "I am going to marry a man named Ellerby. And I expect I'll make his life miserable."

He said teasingly, "Does a girl shed tears when she mentions the name of a man she really plans to marry? I've made you cry many a time, but—"

He was beside her, and she clung as his arms went around her. He kissed her until she fought for breath.

"Not Ellerby, whoever he is, my darling. But me. Because I love you. When the roads are passable—soon, soon—I'll take you away and you'll not need to set foot on the ground or look at—anything."

"No, Joe, not you. Mr. Ellerby will come for me when I write him, and he will hate every mile of it. And I will marry him because he doesn't deserve any better."

"That's nonsense," Doc Frail said. "You will marry me."

Across the street, a man with a bad cold knocked at Doc's door. He kept a handkerchief to his face as he coughed out his message to Rune:

"Can Doc come, or you? Tall John's cut his leg with an axe, bleeding bad."

"I'll come," gasped Rune, and grabbed for Doc's bag. He knew pretty well what to do for an axe cut; he had been working with Doc all winter. "Tell Doc—he's right across the street."

"Go to Tall John's place," the coughing man managed to advise. As far as Rune knew, he went across the street to call Doc. Rune did not look back; he was running to save his patient.

When he was out of sight, another man who had been standing in the shadows pounded on Elizabeth's door, calling frantically, "Doc, come quick! That kid Rune's been stabbed at the Big Nugget!"

He was out of sight when Doc Frail barged out, hesitated a moment, decided he could send someone for his bag, and ran toward the saloon.

He tripped and, as he fell, something hit him on the back of the head.

He did not lie in the mud very long. Two men solicitously carried him back in the opposite direction and laid him in the slush at the far side of Flaunce's store. They left him there and went stumbling down the street, obviously drunk.

Frenchy Plante did not use force in entering Elizabeth's cabin. He knocked and called out, "Miss Armistead, it's Frenchy." In a lower tone, he added, "I got good news for you!"

She opened the door and demanded, "Is Rune hurt badly? Oh, what happened?"

"The boy got hurt?" Frenchy was sympathetic.

"Someone called Dr. Frail to look after him—didn't you see him go?"

Frenchy said good-humoredly, "Miss, I'm too plumb damn excited. Listen, can I come in and show you what I brought?"

She hesitated, too concerned to care whether he came in or not.

"Remember," he whispered, "what I said once about Solid Gold Frenchy?"

She remembered and gasped. "Come in," she said.

Doc reeled along the street, cold, soaking wet, and with his head splitting. He would have stopped long enough to let his head stop spinning, but he was driven by cold fear that was like sickness.

What about Elizabeth alone in her cabin? Where was Rune and how badly was he hurt? Doc was bruised and aching, tricked and defeated. Who had conquered him was not very important. Skull Creek would know soon enough that someone had knocked the starch out of Doc Frail without a shot being fired.

Rune, wherever he was, would have to wait for help if he needed it.

At Elizabeth's door Doc listened and heard her

voice between tears and laughter: "I don't believe it! I don't think it's really true!"

The door was not barred. He opened it and stood watching with narrowed eyes. Elizabeth was rolling something crookedly across the table, something yellow that looked like a small, misshapen apple. When it fell and boomed on the floor boards, he knew what it was.

He asked in a controlled voice, "Has the kid been here?"

Elizabeth glanced up and gasped. She ran to him crying, "Joe, you're hurt—what happened? Come sit down. Oh, Joe!"

Frenchy Plante was all concern and sympathy. "My God, Doc, what hit you?"

Doc Frail brushed Elizabeth gently aside and repeated, "Has the kid been here?"

"Ain't seen him," Frenchy said earnestly. "Miss Armistead was saying you'd been called out, he was hurt, so we thought you was with him."

Doc turned away without answering. He ran, stumbling, toward the Big Nugget. He stood in the doorway of the saloon, mud-stained, bloody and arrogant. He asked in a voice that did not need to be loud, "Is the kid in here?"

Nobody answered that, but someone asked, "Well, now, what happened to you?" in a tone of grandfatherly indulgence.

They were watching him, straight-faced, without concern, without much interest, the way they would look at any other man in camp. But not the way they should have looked at Doc Frail. There was nothing unusual in their attitudes, except that they were not surprised. And they should have been. They expected this, he understood.

"I was informed," Doc said, "that Rune had been knifed in a fight here."

The bartender answered, "Hell, there ain't been a fight here. And Rune ain't been in since he came for you two-three days ago."

Doc was at bay, as harmless as an unarmed baby. He turned to the door and heard laughter, instantly choked.

Outside, he leaned against the wall, sagging, waiting for his head to stop spinning, waiting for his stomach to settle down.

There was danger in the laughter he had heard. And there was nothing he could do. Frail, Frail, Frail.

He realized that he was standing on the spot where Wonder Russell stood when Dusty Smith shot him, long ago.

He began to run, lurching, toward Elizabeth's cabin.

She was waiting in the doorway. She called anxiously, "Joe! Joe!"

Frenchy said, "I kept telling her you'd be all right, but I figured it was best to stay here with her in case anything else happened."

Doc did not answer but sat down, staring at him, and waited for Elizabeth to bring a pan of water and towels. "Is Rune all right?" she demanded.

"I presume so. It was only a joke, I guess."

Golden peas and beans were on the table with the little golden apple. When Doc would not let Elizabeth help him clean the blood off his face, she turned toward the table slowly as if she could not help it.

"He named the mine for me," she whispered. "He calls it the Lucky Lady." Her face puckered, but she did not cry. She laughed instead, choking.

Rune came in at that moment, puzzled and furious, with Doc's bag.

"They said Tall John was hurt," he blurted out, and stopped at sight of Doc Frail.

"The way I heard it," Doc said across the towel, "you were knifed at the saloon. And somebody hit me over the head."

Rune seemed not to hear him. Rune was staring at the nuggets, moving toward them, pulled by the same force that had pulled Elizabeth.

Frenchy chortled, "Meet the Lucky Lady, kid. I got a strike, and half of it is hers. I'll be leaving now. No, the nuggets are yours, Miss, and there'll be more. Sure hope you get over that crack on the head all right, Doc."

Doc's farewell to Elizabeth was a brief warning: "Bar the door. From now on, there'll be trouble."

He did not explain. He left her to think about it.

She did not go to bed at all that night. She sat at the table, fondling the misshapen golden apple and the golden peas and beans, rolling them, counting them.

She held them in her cupped hands, smiling, staring, but not dreaming yet. Their value was unknown to her; there would be plenty of time to get them weighed. They were only a token, anyway. There would be more, lots more.

She hunted out, in its hiding place, a letter she had written to Mr. Ellerby, read it through once, and burned it in the stove.

The golden lumps would build a wall of safety between her and Mr. Ellerby, between her and everything she didn't want.

She sat all night, or stood sometimes by the front window, smiling, hearing the sounds she recognized although she had never heard the like before: the endless racket of a gold rush. Horses' hoofs and the slogging feet of men, forever passing, voices earnest or anxious or angry, the creak of wagons. She listened eagerly with the golden apple cupped in her hand.

Even when someone pounded on her door, she was not afraid. The walls are made of gold, she thought. Nobody can break them down. A man called anxiously, "Lucky Lady, wish me luck! That's all I want, lady, all in the world I want."

Elizabeth answered, "I wish you luck, whoever you are," and laughed.

But when, toward morning, she heard an angry racket outside the back door, she was frightened for Rune. She ran to listen.

"I've got a gun on you," he was raging. "Git going, now!" And men's voices mumbled angrily away. She spoke to him through the closed back door.

"Rune, go and get Doc. I have been making plans."

The three of them sat at the table before dawn. Coffee was in three cups, but only Rune drank his.

Doc listened to Elizabeth and thought, This is some other woman, not the lost lady, the helpless prisoner. This is the Lucky Lady, an imprisoned queen. This is royalty. This is power. She has suddenly learned to command.

"I would like to hire you, Rune, to be my guard," she began.

Rune glanced at Doc, who nodded. Rune did not answer. Elizabeth did not expect him to answer.

"I would like you to buy me a gold scale as soon as possible," she continued. "And please find out from Mr. Flaunce what would be the cost of freighting in a small piano from the States."

Doc said wearily, "Elizabeth, that's defeat. If you order a piano and wait for it to get here, that means you're not even thinking of leaving Skull Creek."

"When I thought of it, thinking did me no good," she answered, and dismissed the argument.

"Rune, please ask Mr. Flaunce to bring over whatever bolts of dress material he has—satin, in a light gray. I shall have a new dress."

Rune put down his coffee cup. "You could build a lean-to on the back here. I'd ought to stay pretty close, and I don't hanker to sleep on that woodpile often."

She nodded approval. "And another thing: grubstaking Frenchy brought me luck. Other miners will think of the same thing, and I will grubstake them, to keep my luck."

Rune growled, "Nonsense. Hand out a stake to every one that asks for it, and you'll be broke in no time. Set a limit—say every seventh man that asks. But don't let anybody know it's the seventh that gets it."

Elizabeth frowned, then nodded. "Seven is a lucky number."

Doc picked up his cup of cool coffee.

A handful of gold has changed us all, he thought. Elizabeth is the queen—the golden Queen Elizabeth. Rune is seventeen years old, but he is a man of sound judgment—and he is the second best shot in the territory. And I, I am a shadow.

Doc said gently, "Elizabeth, there may not be very much more gold for Frenchy to divide with you. You are planning too much grandeur."

"There will be a great deal more," she contradicted, serenely. "I am going to be very rich. I am the Lucky Lady."

9

At the end of a single week, the fragility of the Skull Creek gold camp was plain. The town was collapsing, moving to the new strike at Plante Gulch.

The streets swarmed and boomed with strangers—

but they were only passing through. Flaunce's store was open day and night to serve prospectors replenishing grub supplies and going on to the new riches. Flaunce was desperately trying to hire men to freight some of his stock on to the new diggings to set up another store before someone beat him to it.

Doc Frail lounged in his own doorway waiting for Rune to come from Elizabeth's cabin, and watched the stream of men passing by—bearded, ragged, determined men on foot or on horseback, leading donkeys or mules, driving bull teams with laden wagons, slogging along with packs on their shoulders. Almost all of them were strangers.

Let's see if I'm what I used to be, Doc thought, before Frenchy tricked me and got me hit over the head.

He stepped forward into the path of a pack-laden man, who was walking fast and looking earnestly ahead. When they collided, Doc glared at him with his old arrogance, and the man said angrily, "Damn you, stay out of the way," shoved with his elbow, and went on.

No, I am not what I used to be, Doc admitted silently. The old power, which had worked even on strangers, was gone, the challenge in the stare that asked, Do you amount to anything?

Rune came weaving through the crowd, and Doc saw in him power that was new. Rune looked taller. He wore new, clean clothing and good boots, although the gun in his holster was one Doc had given him months before. Rune was no longer sullen. He wore a worried frown, but he was sure of himself.

Doc pointed with his thumb to a vacant lot, and Rune nodded. It was time for his daily target practice, purposely public. In the vacant space where nobody would get hurt, Doc tossed an empty can, and Rune punctured it with three shots before it fell. The steady stream of passing men became a whirlpool, then stopped, and the crowd grew.

Someone shouted, "Hey, kid," and tossed another can. Doc's pistol and Rune's thundered a duet, and the crowd was pleased.

When Rune's gun was empty, Doc kept firing, still with his right hand but with his second gun, tossed with a flashing movement from his left hand as the first weapon dropped to the ground. No more duet, but solo now, by the old master. He heard admiration among the men around them, and that was all to the good. It was necessary that strangers should know the Lucky Lady was well protected. The border shift, the trick of tossing a loaded gun into the hand that released an empty one, was impressive, but Rune had not yet perfected it enough for public demonstration.

That was all there was to the show. The crowd moved on.

"Go take yourself a walk or something," Doc suggested. "I'll watch Elizabeth's place for a while."

"There's a crazy man in town," Rune said. "Did you see him?"

"There are hundreds of crazy men in town. Do you

mean that fanatical preacher with red whiskers? I've been on the edge of his congregation three or four times but never stopped to listen. I wouldn't be surprised if the camp lynched him just to shut him up."

"He scares me," Rune admitted, frowning. "They don't like him, but he gets everybody mad and growling. He don't preach the love of God. It's all hell fire and damnation."

Doc asked, suddenly suspicious, "Has he been to Elizabeth's?"

"He was. I wouldn't let him in. But when I said he was a preacher, she made me give him some dust. She'd like to talk to him, figuring she'd get some comfort. He's not the kind of preacher that ever comforted anybody. Go listen to him when you have time."

"I have more time than I used to," Doc Frail admitted. Two new doctors had come through Skull Creek, both heading for the booming new settlement at Plante Gulch.

Doc had an opportunity to listen to the preacher the next afternoon. The piano player at a dance hall far down the street threw his back out of kilter while trying to move the piano. Doc went down to his shack, gave him some pain killer and with a straight face prescribed bed rest and hot bricks.

The man squalled, "Who'll heat the bricks? And I can't stay in bed—we've moving this shebang to Plante Gulch soon as they finish laying a floor."

"They need a piano player when they get there,"

Doc reminded him. "I'll tell the boss to see to it you get the hot bricks. You are an important fellow, professor."

"Say, guess I am," the man agreed. "Unless they get a better piano player."

Doc left the proprietor tearing his hair because of the threatened delay, then went out to the street. It was crowded with men whose movement had been slowed by curiosity, for across the street on a packing box the red-haired man was preaching.

His eyes were wild, and so were his gestures, and his sermon was a disconnected series of uncompleted threats. He yelled and choked.

"Oh, ye of little faith! Behold I say unto you! Behold a pale horse: and his name that sat on him was Death, and Hell followed with him! Verily, brethren, do not forget hell—the eternal torment, the fire that never dieth. And I heard a great voice out of the temple saying to the seven angels, go your ways, and pour out the vials of the wrath of God upon the earth.

"Lo, there is a dragon that gives power unto the beast, and you worship the dragon and the beast, saying, 'Who is like unto the beast?' And the dragon is gold and the beast is gold, and lo, ye are eternally damned that seek the dragon or the beast."

The preacher was quoting snatches of Revelation, Doc realized, with changes of his own that were not exactly improvements. But gold may be a dragon and a beast, indeed.

A man in the crowd shouted, "Aw, shut up and go

dig yourself some beast!" and there was a roar of approving laughter.

"Remember Sodom and Gomorrah!" screamed the red-haired man. "For their wickedness they were burned—yea, for their sin and evil! Lo, this camp is wicked like unto those two!"

Doc Frail was caught in an impatient eddy in the moving crowd, and someone growled, "Give that horse a lick or we'll never get out of Sodom and on to Gomorrah by dark!"

The preacher's ranting stirred a kind of futile anger in Joe Frail. What makes him think he's so much better than his congregation? Doc wondered. There's a kind of hatred in him.

"A sinful nation," shouted the preacher. "A people laden with iniquity, the seed of evildoers, children that are corrupters. Hear the word of the Lord, ye rulers of Sodom; give ear unto the law of our God, ye people of Gomorrah!"

The Book of the Prophet Isaiah, reflected Joe Frail, who was the son of a minister's daughter. Immediately the red-haired man returned to Revelation:

"There is given unto me a mouth speaking great things, and power is given unto me to continue forty and two months!"

A man behind Joe Frail shouted, "We ain't going to listen that long."

"If any man have an ear, let him hear! He that leadeth into captivity shall go into captivity; he that killeth with the sword must be killed with the sword."

Joe Frail shivered in spite of himself, thinking, And he that killeth with a pistol?

In that moment a man's voice said behind him, *"That is the man,"* and Doc went tense as if frozen, staring at the red-haired madman.

"That's the man I told you about," the voice went on, moving past him. "Crazy as a loon. His name is Grubb."

How could it be? Doc wondered. How could that be the man for whom I'll hang?

After a few days, the madman went on to Plante Gulch.

By August, Elizabeth Armistead was rich and getting richer. The interior log walls of her cabin were draped with yards of white muslin, her furniture was the finest that could be bought in Skull Creek, her piano had been ordered from the East, and she dressed in satin. But only a few men ever saw her, only every seventh man who came to beg a grubstake from the Lucky Lady, and Frenchy Plante when he came to bring her half the cleanup from the mine.

This is Saturday, Doc Frail remembered. Cleanup day at the sluices. Frenchy will be in with the gold. And I will spend the evening with Elizabeth, waiting for him to come. The Lucky Lady hides behind a golden wall.

He found Elizabeth indignantly arguing with Rune.

"Frenchy sent a man to say they have a big cleanup this time," she told Doc. "And they want a man with a reputation to help guard it on the way in. But Rune refuses to go!"

"I don't get paid to guard gold," Rune said. "I hired out to guard you."

"Half of it's mine," she argued.

"And half of it's Frenchy's. He'll look after it. The bank's going to open up whenever he comes. But I'm going to be right here."

Doc said without a smile, "Young lady, you seem to have a sensible fellow on your payroll," and was pleased to see Rune blush.

By George, he thought, that's probably the first decent thing I ever said to him!

"I'll be here, too," Doc promised. "Just making a social call."

He was too restless to sit down and wait. He stood in the doorway, looking out, thinking aloud: "The month is August, Elizabeth. The day is lovely, even in this barren cleft between barren hills. And you are young, and I am not decrepit. But you're a prisoner." He turned toward her and asked gently, "Còme for a walk with me, Elizabeth?"

"No!" she whispered instantly. "Oh, no!"

He shrugged and turned away. "There was a time when you couldn't go because you didn't have any place to go or enough money. Now you can afford to go anywhere, but you've got a pile of nuggets to hide behind."

"Joe, that's not it at all! I can't go now for the same reason I couldn't go before."

“Have you tried, Elizabeth?”

She would not answer.

He saw that Rune was watching him with slitted eyes and cold anger in the set of his mouth.

“Maybe your partner will bring you some new and unusual nuggets,” Doc remarked. “I wonder where he gets them from.”

“From his mine, of course,” Elizabeth answered. Her special nuggets were not in sight, but Doc knew they were in the covered sugar bowl on the table.

“Madam, I beg to differ. The Lucky Lady is a placer operation. Water is used to wash gold cut of dirt and gravel. Most of your nuggets came from there, all right. But—spread them out and I’ll show you.”

Unwillingly, she tipped the sugar bowl. It was packed with gold; she had to pry it out with a spoon. And this was not her treasure, but her hobby, the private collection she kept just because it was so beautiful.

Doc touched a golden snarl of rigid strands. “That’s wire gold, hardened when it cooled. It squeezed through crevices in rock. Rock, Elizabeth. That’s hard-rock gold, not placer, and it never came from diggings within a couple of hundred miles from here. Neither did those sharpened nuggets with bits of quartz still on them. That gold never came from the mine Frenchy named for you.”

Elizabeth stared, fascinated and frightened. “It was in with some other lumps he brought. Where did he get it?”

"He sent for it, to give you. Some men go courting with flowers. Frenchy gives his chosen one imported gold nuggets."

"Don't talk that way! I don't like it."

"I didn't suppose you would, but it was time to tell you."

Frenchy was cleverly succeeding in two purposes: to please Elizabeth and to taunt Joe Frail.

And we are harmless doves, both of us, Doc thought.

"I wish you'd keep those grubstake contracts at the bank," Doc remarked. Four of them were paying off, and some of the others might. "Why keep them in that red box right here in your cabin?"

"Because I like to look at them sometimes," she said stubbornly. "They're perfectly safe. I have Rune to guard me."

Doc smiled with one corner of his mouth, and she hastened to add, "And I have you, too."

"As long as I live, Elizabeth," he said gently.

Rune tried to clear the air by changing the subject. "I hear the preacher, Grubb, is back."

"Then I would like to talk to him," said Elizabeth. "If he comes to the door, please let him in."

"No!" Doc said quite loudly. "Rune, do not let him in. He's a lunatic."

Elizabeth said coolly, "Rune will let him in. Because I want to talk to him. And because I say so!"

Doc said, "Why, Elizabeth!" and looked at her in astonishment. She sat stiff-backed with her chin high, pale with anger, imperious—the queen behind the golden wall, the Lucky Lady, who had forgotten how vulnerable she was. Doc Frail, newly vulnerable and afraid since the great joke Frenchy played on him, could not stare her down.

"Rune," he began, but she interrupted, "Rune will let him in because I say so."

Rune looked down at them both. "I will not let him in, and not because Doc says to keep him out. I won't let him in—because he shouldn't get in. And that's how it is."

Doc smiled. "The world has changed, Elizabeth. That's how it is. Rune holds all the winning cards—and nobody needs to tell him how to play them."

Rune guessed dimly in that moment that, no matter how long he lived or what he accomplished to win honor among men, he would never be paid any finer compliment.

"Guess I'll go see what's doing around town," he said, embarrassed.

"Both of you can go!" Elizabeth cried in fury.

To her surprise, Doc answered mildly, "All right," and she was left alone. The nuggets from the sugar bowl were scattered on the table. She touched them, fondled them, sorted them into heaps according to size and shape. She began to forget anger and imprisonment. She began to forget that she was young and far from home.

Doc Frail was only a hundred yards away from the cabin when a messenger on a mule hailed him: "Hey,

Doc! My partner Frank's hurt up at our mine. There's three men trying to get him out, or hold up the timbering anyway."

He flung himself off the mule and Doc, who had his satchel, leaped into the saddle. He knew where the mine was.

"Send some more men up there," he urged, and started for it.

Rune, strolling, saw him go and turned at once back to the Lucky Lady's cabin. He did not go in. He hunkered down by the front door and began to whittle.

Down beyond the Big Nugget, the red-haired man was preaching a new sermon, lashing himself to fury—and attracting a more favorably inclined audience than usual. His topic was the Lucky Lady. There was no more fascinating topic in Skull Creek, for she was young and desirable and mysterious, and she represented untold riches, even to men who had never seen her, who knew her only as a legend.

"Lo, there is sin in this camp, great sin!" Grubb was intoning. "The sin that locketh the door on deliverance, that keepeth a young woman prisoner against her will. There is a wicked man who shutteth her up in a cabin, that she escape not, and putteth a guard before her door that righteousness may not enter!"

His listeners were strangers. They believed him, because why not?

One nudged another and murmured, "Say, did you know that?" The other shook his head, frowning.

"She cannot be delivered from evil," intoned Grubb,

"because evil encompasseth her round about. She has no comfort within those walls because the servant of the Lord is forbidden to enter."

Someone asked, "Did you try?"

Grubb had tried just once, weeks earlier. But he remembered it as today, and anger was renewed in him. He began to yell.

"Verily, the servant of the Lord tried to enter, to pray with her for deliverance, to win her from evil. But the guard at the door turned him away and bribed him with nuggets. Lo, the guard was as evil as the master, and both of them are damned!"

His audience saw what he saw, the arrogant doctor who would not let the Lucky Lady go, and the young man who idled at her doorway to keep rescuers away. His audience stirred and murmured, and someone said, "By damn, that's a bad thing!" His audience increased, and Grubb, for once delivering a message to which men listened without reviling him, went on screaming words that he convinced himself were true.

One man on the edge of the crowd walked away—the horse thief who was a friend of Tall John, and of Doc who had cured him, and of Rune who had nursed him. The horse thief passed the barbershop and observed that Frenchy Plante was inside, getting his hair cut. Frenchy's mule was hitched in front, and the gold from the weekly cleanup was no doubt in the pack on the mule. But Frenchy was watching from the barber chair with a rifle across his knees, so the horse thief did not linger.

Walking fast, but not running, he paused in front of the Lucky Lady's cabin and spoke quietly to Rune:

"The red-haired fellow is raising hell, working the men up. Saying the girl could get away if it wasn't Doc pays you to keep her locked up. Don't act excited, kid. We're just talking about the weather. I think there's going to be hell to pay, and I'll go tell Tall John. Where's Doc?"

"Went on a call, on Tim Morrison's mule—to Tim's mine, I guess. Thanks."

Unhurried, Rune entered the Lucky Lady's cabin and sat down.

The horse thief, who did not happen to possess a horse just then, went to the livery stable and rented one. At a trot, he rode to the place where Tall John was washing gravel. Tall John dropped his pick and said, "Go look for Doc." He himself started back toward Elizabeth's cabin at a brisk limp.

Tall John observed that a fairly large crowd had gathered down beyond the Big Nugget, and occasionally a shout came from it.

If they ever get into her cabin, he told himself, they'll have to kill the boy first—and if that happens, she won't care to live either. He and I, between us, will have to keep Frenchy out. Heaven forbid that he should be her rescuer!

Tall John knocked on Elizabeth's door and after he identified himself, Rune let him in. He sat down to chat as if he had come only for a friendly visit.

The horse thief met Doc Frail walking. The man

trapped in the cave-in had died. He was still trapped.

"There's trouble," the horse thief said bluntly, and told him what the trouble was.

"I'll take that horse, please," Doc replied. He rode at a trot; he did not dare attract attention by going faster. And he did not know what he was going to do when he got to the cabin—if he got there.

It is too late to try to take her out of Skull Creek now, he realized. I wonder how much ammunition Rune has. I haven't much—and what can I do with it anyway, except to shoot through the roof and make a noise?

He heard Frenchy shout "Hey Doc!" from down the street, but he did not turn.

The crowd beyond the Big Nugget was beginning to stir and to scatter on the edges. Rune, watching from a peephole in the blanket on the window, let Doc in before he had a chance to knock.

The three inside the cabin were still as statues. Elizabeth said, "They've just told me. Joe, I'll go out when they come in and I'll tell Grubb it isn't so."

"You'll stay right here," Doc answered. "I hope you will not think I am being melodramatic, but I have to do something that I have been putting off for too long. Tall John, can I make a legal will by telling it to you? There's not time to write it. I want to watch that window."

Elizabeth gasped.

Tall John said, "Tell me. I will not forget."

"My name is Joseph Alberts. I am better known as

Joseph Frail. I am of sound mind but in imminent danger of death. I bequeath two thousand dollars in clean gulch gold to—Rune, what's your name?"

Rune answered quietly, "Leonard Henderson."

"To Leonard Henderson, better known as Rune, to enable him to get a medical education if he wants it. Everything else I leave to Elizabeth Armistead, called the Lucky Lady."

"Oh, so lucky!" she choked.

He did not say that he wanted Rune to take her away from Skull Creek. It was not necessary.

"That mob is getting noisier," Doc commented. "Tall John, you'd better go out by the back door."

"I will not forget," Tall John promised. He left the cabin, not stopping even to shake hands.

Just outside the window, Frenchy shouted, "Lucky Lady! I got gold for you! Open the door for Frenchy, Lucky Lady."

No one inside the cabin moved. No one outside could see in.

Frenchy hiccuped and said, "Aw, hell, she ain't home." He rode on, then shouted, "But she's always home, ain't she?"

Doc spoke rapidly. "If I go out this door, both of you stay inside—and bar it. Do you understand?"

"I get it," Rune replied. Elizabeth was crying quietly.

Frenchy's voice came back. "Doc, you in there? Hey, Doc Frail! Come on out. You ain't scared, are you?"

Joe Frail went tense and relaxed with an effort of will.

"You wouldn't shoot me, would you, Doc?" Frenchy teased. "You wouldn't shoot nobody, would you, Doc?" He laughed uproariously, and Doc Frail did not move a muscle.

He heard the muttering mob now, the deep, disturbed murmur that he had heard from the hill on the day the road agent swung from a bough of the great tree.

He heard a shrill scream from Grubb, who saw Frenchy coaxing at the window and had seen Frenchy enter the cabin before.

Grubb's topic did not change, but his theme did, as he led his congregation. His ranting voice reached them:

"Wicked woman! Wicked and damned! Will all your gold save you from hell fire? Wanton and damned—"

Doc forgot he was a coward. He forgot a man lying dead in Utah. He forgot Wonder Russell, sleeping in a grave on the hill. He slammed the bar upward from the door and stepped into the street.

His voice was thunder: "Grubb, get down on your knees!"

Grubb was blind to danger. He did not even recognize Doc Frail as an obstacle. Clawing the air, he came on, screaming, "Babylon and the wicked woman—"

Doc Frail gasped and shot him.

He did not see Grubb fall, for the mob's wrath downed him. The last thing he heard as he went down under the deluge was the sound he wanted to hear: the bar falling shut inside the cabin door.

10

The rabble. The rabble. The first emotion he felt was contempt. Fear would come later. But no; fear had come. His mouth was cotton-dry.

He was bruised and battered, had been unconscious. He could not see the men he heard and despised. He lay face down on dirty boards and could see the ground through a crack. On a platform? No, his legs were bent and cramped. He was in a cart. He could not move his arms. They were bound to his body with rope.

The rabble shouted and jeered, but not all the jeering was for him—they could not agree among themselves. He knew where he was; under the hanging tree.

A voice cried furiously, "A trial! You've got to give the man a trial!"

Another shout mounted: "Sure, try him—he shot the preacher!"

This is the place and this is the tree, Joe Frail understood, and the rope must be almost ready. Grubb was the man, and I hardly knew he existed.

There was nothing that required doing. Someone else would do it all. There was something monstrous to be concerned about—but not for long.

And there was Elizabeth.

Joe Frail groaned and strained at the rope that bound him, and he heard Frenchy laugh.

"Let the boys see you, Doc," Frenchy urged. "Let 'em have a last good look!"

Someone heaved him to his feet and he blinked through his hair, fallen down over his eyes. The mob turned quiet, staring at a man who was as good as dead.

There was no need for dignity now, no need for anything. If he swayed, someone supported him. If he fell, they would stand him on his feet again. Everything that was to be done would be done by someone else. Joe Frail had no responsibilities any more. (Except—Elizabeth? Elizabeth?)

"Hell, that's no decent way to do it," someone argued with authority, not asking for justice but only for a proper execution. "The end of the cart will catch his feet that way. Put a plank across it. Then he'll get a good drop."

There was busy delay while men streamed down the hill to get planks.

Joe Frail threw back his head with the old arrogant gesture and could see better with his hair tossed away from his eyes. He could see Skull Creek better than he wanted to, as clearly as when he first walked under the tree with Wonder Russell.

Elizabeth, Elizabeth. He was shaken with anger. When a man is at his own hanging, he should not have to think of anyone but himself.

And still, he understood, even now Joe Frail must fret helplessly about Elizabeth. Who ever really died at peace except those who had nothing to live for?

Men were coming with planks—four or five men, four or five planks. They busied themselves laying planks across the cart to make a platform so they could take satisfaction in having hanged him decently and with compassion. And from the side, Frenchy was bringing up a team of horses to pull the cart away.

Someone behind him slipped a noose down over his head, then took it off again, testing the length of the rope. Above, someone climbed along the out-thrust bough of the tree to tie it shorter. Joe Frail stood steady, not looking up, not glancing sideways at the horses being urged into position.

The crowd was quieter now, waiting.

Just as the team came into position in front of the cart, he saw movement down in the street of Skull Creek and strained forward.

Elizabeth's door had opened and Rune had come out of her cabin.

No! No! You damn young fool, stay in there and do what you can to save her! By tomorrow, they'll slink off like dogs and you can get her away safely. You fool! You utter fool!

What's he carrying? A red box.

No, Elizabeth! Oh, God, not Elizabeth! Stay in the cabin! Stay out of sight!

But the Lucky Lady had emerged from her refuge and was walking beside Rune. Walking fast, half running, with her head bent. Don't look, Elizabeth! My darling, don't look up! Turn back, turn back to the cabin. Tomorrow you can leave it.

A man behind Doc remarked, "Well, would you look at that!" but nobody else seemed to notice.

Doc said sharply, "What the hell are you waiting for?" Suddenly he was in a hurry. If they finished this fast enough, she would go back—Rune would see to it.

She was leaning forward against the wind of the desert that was thirty miles away. She was stumbling. But she did not fall. She had got past Flaunce's store.

The red box Rune is carrying? The box she keeps her gold in. Go back. Go back.

Someone slipped the noose down over his head again and he groaned and was ashamed.

She was struggling up the first slope of the barren hill, fighting the desert. Her right arm was across her eyes. But Doc could see Rune's face. Rune was carrying the heavy box and could not help the Lucky Lady, but the look on his face was one Doc had seen there seldom. It was pity.

The team was ready, the platform was prepared, the noose was around the condemned man's neck. The Lucky Lady stopped halfway up the hill.

There was almost no sound from the rabble except their breathing. Some of them were watching Elizabeth. She lifted her right hand and fired a shot from the derringer into the air.

Then they all watched her. The silence was complete

and vast. The men stared and waited.

Rune put the red box on the ground and opened it, handed something to Elizabeth—a poke, Doc thought. She emptied it into her hand and threw nuggets toward the silent mob.

No one moved. No one spoke or even murmured. Why, Rune has no gun, Doc saw. It is a long time since I have seen him with no holster on his hip. And Elizabeth has fired into the air the one shot her pistol will hold. They are unarmed, helpless. As helpless as I am.

The voice he heard was his own, screaming, "Go back! Go back!"

A man behind him rested a hand on his shoulder without roughness, as if to say, Hush, hush, this is a time for silence.

Elizabeth stooped again to the box and took out something white—the sugar bowl. She flung the great, shining nuggets of her golden treasure, two and three at a time, toward the motionless men on the slope. Then they were not quite motionless, there was jerky movement among them, instantly ceasing, as they yearned toward the scattered treasure but would not yield.

Elizabeth stood for a while with her head bent and her hands hanging empty. Joe Frail saw her shoulders move as she gulped in great breaths of air. Rune stood watching her with that look of pity twisting his mouth.

She bent once more and took out a folded paper, held it high, and gave it to the wind. It sailed a little distance before it reached the ground. She waited with her head bowed, and the mob waited, stirring with the restless motion of puzzled men.

She tossed another paper and another. Someone asked the air a question: "Contracts? Grubstake contracts?" And someone else said, "But which ones?"

Most of the contracts had no meaning any more, but a very few of them commanded for the Lucky Lady half the golden treasure that sifted out of paying mines.

Frenchy's voice roared with glee: "She's buying Doc Frail! The Lucky Lady is buying her man!"

Joe Frail quivered, thinking, This is the last indignity. She has gambled everything, and there will be nothing for her to remember except my shame.

All the contracts, one at a time, she offered to the mob, and the wind claimed each paper for a brief time. All the nuggets in the sugar bowl. All the pale dust in the little leather bags that made the red box heavy.

Elizabeth stood at last with her hands empty. She touched the box with her foot and Rune lifted it, turned it upside down to show that it held nothing more, and let it fall.

Frenchy's shout and Frenchy's forward rush broke the mob's indecision. He yelled, "Come and git it, boys! Git your share of the price she's paying for Doc Frail!"

Frenchy ran for the scattered papers, tossed away one after another, then held one up, roaring, and kissed it.

The rabble broke. Shouting and howling, the mob scattered, the men scrabbled for gold in the dust. They swarmed like vicious ants, fighting for the treasure.

A jeering voice behind Doc said, "Hell, if she wants you that bad!" and cut the rope that bound him. The knife slashed his wrist and he felt blood run.

The Lucky Lady was running up the slope to him, not stumbling, not hesitating, free of fear and treasure, up toward the hanging tree. Her face was pale, but her eyes were shining.